The Word for Moving Clouds

14 Stories from the Red Shed

edited by
John Irving Clarke

cover design by
Mike Barrett

Currock Press

First published in 2017 by Currock Press
3, Sandal Cliff, Sandal, Wakefield, WF2 6AU
www.currockpress.com

ISBN 978-0-9575422-8-0

Copyright ©in all cases remains with the authors
Editorial selection © John Irving Clarke 2017

The right of John Irving Clarke to be identified as the editor of this work has been asserted in accordance with the Copyright, Designs and Patents Act 1988.

All rights reserved. No part of this publication may be reproduced, stored in or introduced into a retrieval system, or transmitted in any form by any means (electronic, mechanical, photocopying, recording or otherwise) without prior written permission from the rights holders.

A CIP record for this book is available from the British Library.

Printed and bound in Great Britain by CMP
cmpbookprinting.co.uk

The Word for Moving Clouds

14 Stories from the Red Shed

Dedication

This book is dedicated to the troubadours: the poets, performers and musicians who have appeared at the Red Shed Readings; it is dedicated to the open mic readers and the audience members who contribute so tellingly to the event; and to the guest artists who turn up and invariably say, "It *is* a shed, and it *is* red!"

Most of all, this book is dedicated to Jimmy Andrex, who provides the energy and verve.

Contents

Introduction, 9
Circular Saw Refresher Course, Jimmy Andrex, 11
Things that are Lost and were Broken, S.J. Bradley, 21
Poppy Jones and the Ding Dong Song, John Irving Clarke, 29
Cheshire Life, Steve Dearden, 37
The Girl of Lake Silver, Berlie Doherty, 47
Putting the Fun back in Funeral, Gareth Durasow, 55
Just hours before he became a saint, Ian McMillan, 63
Mermaid, Silvia Pio, 69
Chatterley, Laura Potts, 75
The Miller's Tale, Richard Smyth, 83
Excerpt from Storybank: The Milkfarm Years, Jane Steele, 89
Elephant Gin, Michael Stewart, 97
The fellow from whom came the sea, Matthew Hedley Stoppard, 107
Welcome to Horbury, William Thirsk-Gaskill, 113
Authors' biographies, *123*

Introduction

Like all great ideas, it was deceptively simple: why not ask those writers who have appeared under The Red Shed Readings banner to donate a prose piece to an anthology celebrating the tenth year of the Readings?

It was a simple plan but it has proved to be so rewarding. From the outset, the scheme was marked by the enthusiasm and creativity of the writers involved. There was a limit of 2,000 words imposed but no restriction on style or theme, and the writers revelled in such freedom. Read for yourself these stories of heroes and villains, of love lost and found, of dystopian futures and magical pasts; read for yourself the eclectic take on the human plight. Read and enjoy.

I would like to extend my personal thanks to the National Association of Writers Groups and to Keely Hodgson of the Purple Room Poetry at Ben Rhydding, whose generosity has enabled this simple plan to take shape. Thanks are also due to all those who have worked tirelessly behind the scenes on this book and at the Red Shed Readings.

The proof of the pudding… they say. Well, it's time to pick up your spoons.

John Irving Clarke, 2017

Circular Saw Refresher Course

Jimmy Andrex

The one-time family prodigy cleared his throat, brushed skin flakes from viscose lapels and straightened his Daffy Duck tie.

"OK, Gents. The sooner we get started…. Welcome to the 3 Year Statutory Circular Saw Refresher Course here at Hemsworth Kaizen Professional Development Hub."

Formerly a music room thrown up in 1974 to cater for the raising of the school leaving age its function now seemed to be the collection of flat footballs and rainwater, which dripped routinely into a bucket under an empty notice board entitled OPPORTUNITIES.

His audience blearily shuffled into a loose semi-circle, some still dunking a last digestive into foam cups. Nicotine eyebags were worn like long service medals. Veterans of years of classroom firefights, they had lovingly honed world-weariness into an art form.

"As you are all aware, this course is a requirement for all professionals working with young people in a workshop environment which aims to reinforce basic…"

Already, he'd lost them. Their thousand yard stare already lured away to the patch of tarmac between portakabins which had evolved into a car park. Absent minds were a weary multiplex of sporting near-misses, pyhrric victories over pre-teens and unfeasible sexual fantasies. He hated these courses. Most present were here for their fourth or fifth time. So, with little to lose, he resorted to his latest joke someone had sent him on Facebook.

"…ensuring that whenever the guard is raised, mains power is isolated at the…er…mains. Speaking of mains power: Why does it take three women with PMT to change a lightbulb?"

A threatening silence followed by a percussive nasal exhalation was as near to encouragement as he was going to get, so he ploughed on.

"IT JUST DOES. ALRIGHT?"

One spilled his tea and half a dozen shoulders relaxed. Karl Jung often spoke of the power of the collective subconscious having the potential to bind people together through humour, but what he'd have made of this sullen gamelan of tapering snorts is anyone's guess. Then again, he wasn't escaping the tedium of delivering GCSE Resistant Materials by delivering In Service Training. Or was it Common Professional Development? They kept changing it.

The limp ovation encouraged Colin to spread his performance wings a little, faced as he was with spinning out a whole day telling a semi-hostile crowd what they already knew, namely:

1. Circular saws cut things and they fucking hurt.
2. Don't let anyone cut their hand off.
3. Put the guard down.

He could have measured their previous understanding as soon as they arrived by asking them to hold up their hands and count. So, on a roll, he went back to the comedy. This time he'd do his accents:

"There's a Frenchman, and Italian and a bloke from Seacroft in a bar talking about sex. The Frenchman says; when I make love to my woman, she is so in ze ecstasy zat she levitate 5 centimetres above ze bed."

Catatonic gazes gave him the green light to continue.

"The Italian goes; when I make-ah da love to ma wife-ah, she levitate 10 centimetres above ah da bed-ah."

They anticipated the payoff like a firing squad.

"The bloke from Seacroft says; When I've just shagged our lass, I wipe me knob on t'curtains and she hits the fuckin roof."

SCREEEEEEEEEEEEEEEEEEEEEEEEEEEEEEEEEEEEEEE
EEEEEEEEEEEEEEE

His punchline was lost as his audience swivelled like tweed meerkats. The saw, dormant until now, seemed to have started spontaneously, the only one in the room to get the gag. However, as Ken-the-Technician sloped in from the workshop where he'd been bagging up the kindling he sold at the end of his drive, it transpired that he'd knocked the master isolator switch next door exposing those present to the previously undocumented hazard of Bored-Teacher-Leaning-Against-On-Switch.

Gamely, Colin attempted to reassert his manhood.

"Ah…Gents, that sketch is better than a thousand words."

At this point, Colin's world, unmoored by adrenaline, began to break apart like a beached coaster.

"Are we going to stand here listening to this inadequate rubbish all day or are we going to DO something?" mithered a twenty-something in a Jeff Banks suit seemingly at odds with his 2cm lobe-stretching ring until you bore in mind that teacher burnout rates gave rise to a promotion culture unseen since the Allied invasion of Italy. Anyone now left standing in a classroom unaided stood a 70-30 chance of being promoted in their first year. He had, and now he was living the dream.

"Come on, I could be filling in my Progress Conversation Sheets instead of listening to this, plus I've got Leadership Cabinet Moot at 3, so I need to be off."

"Oi, Hipster, leave it out. This is the first time I've had a day out in ages. All I've got to go back to is some Senior Leadership child going through a spreadsheet so tiny I can't even read it me as part of my Difficulties Plan. Can't we just chop stuff up, like we always do?" vented Year-Head-With-Two-Kids-At-University.

"Fair enough, but why do we have to be here at all?" ventured Ponytail-Beard-And-Rugby-Shirt.

"This is a typical Tory waste of time and money."

This was the cue for Former-Life-And-Soul-Caring-For-Mother-With-Dementia to attempt to pour oil on the already polluted waters.

"Hold on, hold on, we don't need this, his patter's a bit lame, granted, but at least he's not telling us about his parents and career achievements for an hour like our Executive Head always does. Give him a break."

Colin's train of thought derailed from trying to remember what exactly the C stood for in CPD to seize his moment. This might be his career death twitches, but it was better than what he had planned.

"Look, if that's your general feeling, why don't we just spend an hour trying to break the blade then write it up as a risk-assessment exercise to keep our Heads happy, break early for lunch then use the time to catch up on our admin?"

He had uttered the magic words. Lunch. Early. Admin. The atmosphere lurched giddily from torpor to purpose in a heartbeat.

Ponytail-Beard-And-Rugby-Shirt was galvanised.

"Yeah! Let's feed in thicker stuff just to see what happens!"

Former-Life-And-Soul concurred.

"MDF really fucks them up."

Jeff-Banks-Suit-With-Earlobe-Stretchers was having none of it. "You lot are a disgrace. I'm off to the Interactive Learning Nexus to work on my NQT Standards."

Colin, liberated, felt years younger. Or older. He didn't care which.

"If you mean the Library, it's down the corridor on the right, but don't forget to fill in your evaluation before you go."

Like pardoned murderers they set to with nostalgic zeal, scouring the workshop for materials of ever-increasing unsuitability and risk to toss towards the spinning blade. Plywood chunks made a pleasing ZZZZAAARRRPPP like a Death Ray in a 1940's Flash Gordon serial. Tubular metal chair legs, prised from the pile of broken bits in the corner, proved surprisingly buttery when introduced. Colin, meanwhile, was in the corner, forging Evaluation Questionnaires to keep the ever vigilant gods of Quality Assurance at bay. No-one here was going to blab. Wasn't it C for Central? That was it. Central Professional Development.

But it wasn't.

Eventually, just when it looked like this might be all a pleasant dream from which they had yet to awaken, Year-Head-With-Two-Kids-At-University, had a Eureka moment.

"What about coins?"

"Yeah, who's got some change?"

With a common purpose they would have mistaken for wishful thinking earlier on, the objects materialised. A loose consensus emerged that 2p's represented the optimum damage-for-value ratio.

Ponytail-Beard-And-Rugby-Shirt volunteered for the first shot. Adopting a sideways stance he'd seen during the Olympic Epee coverage on the Red Button, he flexed his legs, breathed deep and aimed. It fell short.

"Come on, William Tell. That was crap."

"It was a sighter," he pleaded.

He addressed the saw then aimed again.

THHHAAAANNNNGGG.

The 2p was spat out like abuse and went airborne. There was a plastic clump and then bafflement. Where was it? Heads rotated.

"Look where it went!" shrieked Former-Life-And-Soul-Caring-For-Mother-With-Dementia, pointing to a tile in the suspended ceiling. The coin was embedded pleasingly in the flame-retardant polystyrene to hoots of glee from the company. Even Colin looked up and grinned. Was it C for Contingent? No.

"Let's try a 50p, come on, I'll stump up," giggled Ponytail-Beard-And-Rugby-Shirt, now in a state of grace he remembered vaguely from about 1983 at Lanchester Polytechnic. He didn't know what they called it now.

Former-Life-And-Soul snatched the coin and, keeping his elbow above the shoulder like he'd been coached as a former league cricketer, he let fly.

THHHHUUUDDDDzzzzzzzzzzzzzzzzzzzbbbbbbbzzzzzzzzbbbbbbbbb

The blade, gulping the meal like a child at a birthday party, had choked.

Punching the off switch, Ponytail-Beard-And-Rugby-Shirt, retrieved the bent coin like a trophy but ruefully noted that the blade remained proud and intact.

"Who's for a pound then, that's bound to do it."

"Go on then."

Jeff-Banks-Suit-With-Earlobe-Stretchers had returned from his self-imposed aspirational exile. Much as he craved advancement, he still saw himself as one-of-the-lads. Fishing the coin from his off-the-peg pocket he punched the start button then side-armed it towards the monster's hungry mouth.

ZINNNNGGGGGGGGGFFFLUBB. Silence.

"Where's it gone?"

"I dunno. I heard a noise but I never saw it."

"Ha ha. You never see the one that gets you, eh?"

"Yeah, but where is it?"

The next ten minutes rolled happily by with speculation, head-scratching and pottering until Colin suddenly sat bolt upright.

"C for CONTINUING. Continuing Professional Development. That's it! Right everyone, I'm giving you permission to go now. Thanks for coming. Enjoy the rest of your day."

The group shrugged, revelled in a final cursory scan for Jeff-Banks-Suit-With-Earlobe-Stretcher's pound then dribbled out. Colin shuffled his papers, muttering under his breath.

"Continuing Professional Development. CPD. That's it. I'll use that in a meeting."

As he closed the door, he turned, remembering it was polite to thank the staff.

"Cheers, Ken."

Any response was lost in the whirr off machinery. Oh well.

Next door, Ken-The-Technician lay, blood seeping from a small wound in the back of his head. A pound coin, purple at the edges by now, lay guilty.

Tails.

Things that are Lost and were Broken

S.J. Bradley

The alarm beeps and beeps in the darkness, the single-note buzz persisting around the walls like an angry digital bee. Paul raises his head slightly from the pillow, feeling insulted. He, lying awake with his eyelids lightly closed in the dull cold air, had thought it was earlier. Under the curtains, night looms between the folds, the heavy curves of the crushed velvet appearing gloomier on the outside than the in. The flashing numbers sear electric turquoise trails in the dark, leaving carved images on his retinas where they came, and went again. Time to get up.

Sinking in the distance, hanging far away over the terraced roofs, the moon still lingers in a midnight-blue sky. Recently night has seemed to last forever, although apparently the sun will always come up. It was there yesterday, and the day before that, the universe disappointing him with its stoic insistence on going through the motions, at a time when he feels as though the very earth might crumble away beneath him. The days assault him with their reliability, turning up one after another and forcing him to endure them, and the most he can do is to keep putting one foot in front of the other.

Not so long ago, Paul had been happy. In the mornings, spurred by a childlike feeling of mild curiosity, he'd leap out of the bed leaving the still-slumbering form inside it, and get ready for work with a song just out of reach of his mouth. Although he hadn't laughed often – he wasn't the type – he had been content. The days were pleasingly smooth, his movements dictated by a more satisfying kind of automation. He went through life in a type of hazy, dreamy contentment, coming home in the afternoons to the smell of pastry and potatoes, and spending the evenings dozing pleasantly in front of the television with his arm loosely around the woman who made it all possible. Things change, the givens go. She went away suddenly, and everything was different after that.

Paul is unremarkably ordinary, and always has been. His mother and father, who lived quietly and obediently in a two-up two-down house in a decent housing estate, rarely argued, and brought him up in an atmosphere of austere satisfaction. Voices were never raised, and disagreements efficiently solved by father, who wrote lists and diagrams, and at the end of his decision-making process, explained logically how he had arrived at his conclusion. Tea was always prompt, and the house tidy. Mother worked part-time in the library, and her habit of speaking quietly, whether in-born or learned, went with her in the house too. His parents showed their affection in understated ways, a touch on the shoulder as the peas were passed, or a chaste embrace in the kitchen after work, communicating in their every movement the value of living an undramatic life.

Paul himself went to a school ten minutes' walk from home, where he gained an impeccable record for attendance. He neither excelled himself enough to be distinguished, and nor did he cause the sort of disruption that drew any attention. His classmates admired his easy-going, blank demeanour, and he was famous for his laconic ability to stay calm in every situation. On the sports field, he was less of a ferocious tiger, and more of an ambling, amiable shire horse. Although not in the popular set, he was well-liked by everyone who met him. When school ended, he took a job with the Highways Agency. It was a grimy, dirty, hot and dangerous job; he liked the camaraderie of it. They worked early and they worked long, Paul putting out the cones as the cars roared by, the roar of engines long in his ears after the day ended. It required little of him besides reliability and the ability to stay calm in the face of danger. It suited him, and he couldn't imagine himself doing anything else. There were four other men in his work-gang, and he had married one of their sisters.

They had first met in the golf club bar, at Gary and Tina's wedding reception. Gary was on the dance floor with his new wife, the rest of them sitting around a table cluttered with empty pint jars. As ever, they were talking about women. That night, there were a lot of them clicking together in small groups. They formed circles, moving their legs and shoulders in time with the music, like herons trying to dislodge a fly. According to custom, Paul and the others were devising a mental league table of the prettiest. When talk turned around to the girl in the violet dress with the stout hips and the broad, large-featured face, Paul said: "Don't say a thing about her. That's my future wife you're talking about." They roared with laughter, and clapped him on the back, and didn't say two more words about it. The champagne had got the better of him.

She turned out to be Gary's sister, two years younger than he, and with a respectable job in the admin department of the local college. Paul's mind was made up the moment he laid eyes on her. Hers took a little longer. Eventually, she suffered him to court her and, in the end, marry her. She insisted on a church wedding and he went along with it. It didn't matter too much to him about the ceremony itself. "What the lady wants, the lady gets," he grumbled to the boys, pretending to mind. Afterwards, he carried his wife over the threshold into this house, with the kitchen in the back room, and the bathroom whose window always needs to be open so that the steam can escape.

He thought they were happy, then one day she said, "I just need some time." Nothing could move him to histrionics, and so he gave it to her. It wasn't in him not to take her words at face value, and he expected her to be back after a week, or maybe two. The days elapsed, the house growing ever louder with her absence. The periods of silence seemed to yawn ever longer, but still he hoped that she might come back. He tried desperately to stay normal, but on the inside was thinking, thinking, thinking. Why did she go? What had he done wrong? Where did she go? Always the same things, never anything useful, over and over again. Every single notion he has repeats itself, his thoughts prowling around in circles, snapping at their own tails like hungry dogs. He would like to wake with a new revelation, except he never sleeps.

The hours no longer flew by, each minute dragging out to unnatural lengths. It was during one of these long days that the box appeared. He had been at work, and it was in the hall when he came in, a fairly small corrugated cardboard box that had once transported several multi-packs of tissues. It had been folded together for the purposes of moving things. The lid was angled open, but there was nothing in it. He picked it up and brought it upstairs.

There was another box the same in the wardrobe, the box of broken things she called it, and he slid this new box in beside it on the shelf. He closed the wardrobe doors and looked around, and saw that her things had gone. It had been her habit to fling her things off when she came in, for them to find their new homes wherever they lay. This was how her gloves came to live by the desk-legs, and her hat on the chest of drawers. Weeks later, when she wanted to wear the flung clothes again, she would rifle the drawers and wardrobe in a fury, declaring that everything was lost, that she could never find anything, and why were things never where they should be? She flew everywhere in a blur of high-pitched noises and colour, always leaving a trail of crumpled clothes in her wake. The only time she was ever quiet was when she was asleep, her face relaxed in slumber, hair curling in dark exclamations all over the pillow. Her smell on the sheets receded weakly into his, now, and he didn't want to wash them. Every now and again he caught the faint scent of shampoo and coffee that was a reminder that she had been there. He was loath to be rid even of these little faint suggestions of her presence. But now, that odd black sock, an old worn greying thing that had long peeked out from underneath the bed, had gone; and she had taken the handbag whose strap had been looped around the banister.

With her detritus removed, the room looked tidier. It looked empty. Often-worn jackets and jumpers had gone from the wardrobe, bottles and jars from the bathroom. The dressing-table was swept clean of brushes and compacts. Even the bed-spread was pulled a little straighter than he had left it when going out. All of her mess had gone, except for the box of broken things, the collection of things she wouldn't hear of throwing away, something over which they had frequently argued. The box held nothing of earthly use or value. The items in it, which no longer served any purpose, lay expired together in a tangle of dead circuit boards and plastic casing. It had begun with the remote control when the buttons stopped working. "It seems wasteful to throw it away," she said, and so it began. The collection expanded every time some small thing gave up the ghost, and came to include, amongst other things, a lighter full of gas but without any flint, a turning corkscrew with one broken arm, and an old pair of curling tongs that no longer reached the temperature required to curl hair.

"What are you going to do with them?" he asked, despairing. Her answers never gave him any satisfaction, and yet he wasn't allowed to throw the things away: she argued fiercely against it. They had such towering rows over this thing and when the insults traded reached a point beyond her tolerance she would shout, half-jokingly, that she was going to start a fucking museum.

He went up from the shower, rubbing his hair with a towel, and stood in front of the open wardrobe.
Now that he had chance to throw it away, he hesitated. Between that

and the unwashed sheets were the memories, the clues that she had been here, and the lingering hope that she might come back. His optimism that all she needed was a few more days, a little more time away, guttered with the buffeting of each passing day. The prospect of her coming home, bags in hand, with an apologetic smile on that large-featured face, never quite went out of his thoughts. He had decided to ask her no questions. If he became too difficult, she could easily leave again. Instead, holding back sobs of gratitude, he would welcome her back with open arms, and pretend that nothing had happened.

It couldn't be gone when she returned. She would notice. Not straight away, but eventually, and then the arguments would start again. It would be weeks before she'd open the wardrobe. Leaving her bag on the floor, in a spot where each would have to walk around it daily, she would unzip the lid and take clothes out of it as she needed them, rather than unpack. Once it was empty, she would open the wardrobe to shove it into the bottom, and then ask, "Where's the box?"

He closed the doors, first the right and then the left, and put on his clothes for work. It would stay in there for another day, and tomorrow again, like today, he would open the doors and look at it and wonder what to do.

Dressed and ready, he pulled at the curtains. Over to the east, in the houses over Graham Road, a thin strip of grey hugged insecurely their roofs and gardens. The sun was rising again. It was time to go to work.

Poppy Jones and the Ding Dong Song

John Irving Clarke

Poppy Jones was my muse, my siren and my next door neighbour. Watching her peg out her washing was a joy; at one with the birdsong and a breezy drying day she'd stand on her tiptoes with a clothes peg in mouth and arch her back to reach the highest line on the dryer. And from my writer's garret, I'd watch.

I'd watch her too when she wheeled her ticking bicycle down the path, when she set out for a run or when she strode purposefully from the house carrying a big brown satchel. There was no apparent routine and no regular pattern as Poppy was a free-spirit blithely unaware of the dictates of timetables, but Monday, I knew was washing day when she'd tiptoe, arch and peg.

She fluttered freely while I twisted in agony. Twisted that is until the day the postman offered my deliverance with a wrongly addressed letter. This called for a neighbourly kindness; it called for me to climb into my suit of chivalrous armour.

"Hi, I'm Robert, Robert Bell from next door and I'm playing postman." I held out the letter and she responded with the deadly combination of direct eye-contact and a smile which could transform winter into spring.

"Robert Bell, the reclusive writer from next door? You'd better come in and have a coffee."

Freshly percolated coffee, funky polka dot mugs and Poppy Jones chatting freely made for a pleasant change to my usual monastic regime.

"So, should I know you? What sort of things do you write? Any of those steamy bodice rippers?" she asked.

The surface truth was much more prosaic: two volumes of verse, no longer in print, a critical study of George Herbert which is almost as difficult to find and a string of reviews for the posh Sundays.

She showed a genuine interest. "Reviewing, does that pay well?"

"On a bad year: no. On a good year: no."

I love it when she laughs.

For her part she did individual music tuition with the talentless wonders of over-rich parents and occasional days in school, interrupting the march of the Gradgrind curriculum for a bit of arts provision box ticking she told me.

"And you run." I said.

"Yes, thank goodness for running; running sets me free. It's where I get my tunes. Have you got a tracksuit? Because if you took up running, that's where you could find your poems."

Now what made her think I needed to look for poems? I changed the subject away from the fearful prospect of grunting and heaving on pavements.

"What do you do with your tunes?"

"Not much. I put a few on-line, I pitch a few to music publishers, but most of them sit in confinement waiting for release."

"That's no kind of life for a tune."

"No, they need to fly; they need some words, I need a lyricist."

The moment was pregnant with possibility but I drained my coffee and left because I was suddenly tempted to tell her about Bobby Chime and confess all.

I was a serious writer and she shouldn't find out about Bobby Chime who was the result of a night of drunken excess. But he was also the benefactor who kept a roof over my head. He kept my body and occasionally my soul, together and had done so since he had met up in a pub with some mates one night while he was at University. It was the night he was told about an upcoming recording session and the final song which was needed for an album. There should be a blue plaque on that pub wall now because that was where Bobby Chime reached for a napkin and wrote down the words to his masterpiece:

"When everything is going wrong
And the whole world begins to mong

Then come and sing our song
Ding dong, ding dong
Come and sing the ding dong song."

These were the lyrics which brought Bob Dylan and Paul Simon to sit cross-legged at his feet in awed respect. Okay, I lied about that last bit and the song didn't go on the album, but it did get recorded and released as a novelty single which flopped miserably. Or at least it did at first but in the curious way that these things happen: word of mouth and becoming a club favourite in European hot-spots, it took off suddenly and all summer it was the tune which was permanently imprinted on everyone's brain. There was a dance created to go with the song, originally a representation of bell ringing but eventually it was the camp in campanology which triumphed.

And that should have been that – one summer in the sun – but a reality t.v. show adopted it as the theme tune and the song became audio shorthand for naffness, the go-to tune for satirists and advertising campaigns where any awareness of irony had been completely removed. Erudite articles were written about the song's unaccountable appeal, some decrying the nation's rock bottom cultural sophistication while others found merit in its complete lack of pretension. One academic lauded "when everything is going wrong/and the whole world begins to mong" as the line with which everyone felt compelled to sing along; the biggest hook since Wet Wet Wet had felt it in their fingers and their toes.

Bobby Chime meanwhile, who had sole rights for the lyrics and a share of performing rights thanks to his sonorous spoken contribution midway through the song: "blow a trumpet, bang a gong/gong, gong, gong, gong, gong," sat back and whistled incredulously every year when he opened his royalty cheque.

But Bobby Chime was an embarrassment and he and Poppy Jones could never meet whereas Poppy and *I* did meet occasionally now: putting out the bins, passing each other as we set out for and returned from the shops when she'd give me a smile which I'd wrap up and take home to enjoy later. And I'd treasure too her little snippets of conversation, nearly always about the importance of writing or composing and the importance of the daily habit.

One day I would invite her inside to repay the cup of coffee I owed her and with this in mind I embarked on a massive spring cleaning of the kitchen and the sitting room. I too could find some trendy mugs. When Poppy Jones did come in to my house it wasn't at a time of my choosing. I was in the back bedroom gazing in awe at the speed with which black cloud could race across the sky to swallow up sunny blue and presage a downpour. When rain was thumping on my widow demanding to be let in I had to finally put down my pen; no one could write through that. Then a hammering on the front door finally convinced me to leave my desk and blunder downstairs to see who on earth could be standing on my doorstep at this time and in this weather.

I had never seen anyone look so disconsolate. "You're wet through." I said with my writer's observational skills bang on the nail.

"I've done something stupid; I've been for a run and locked myself out."

I ushered her in over her protests. A few drops of water in my hallway weren't going to cause a problem.

"I'm dripping everywhere. Have you got a towel I could use?"

I could do much better than that. Offering up a quick prayer of thanks for a newly cleaned bathroom I insisted that she should shower. I could also offer a pile of neatly ironed, folded towels and a fleecy cotton sweat-suit.

"But it will be miles too big for me."

"No, I think it will be just about the right size. It's not mine." She looked at me keenly. "It's surplus to requirements now." I said by way of clumsy explanation and with a nod of understanding she turned and closed the bathroom door between us.

I decided against coffee as this called for a steaming mug of hot chocolate. I had to use a spoon to chip at the chocolate powder which had hardened in the tin but I was going for that special occasion feel: the, *we can make something cosy out of adversity* feel, and the milk still smelled okay.

Let's not beat about the bush. When Poppy Jones walked into the room wearing a borrowed sweat-suit, drying her surprisingly long hair over her shoulder, it was a sight to charge the batteries of any flattened male. Her spirit had returned, she glowed and it wasn't just the fact that I had my hands around a steaming mug of chocolate that I too felt warmed. She took a sip from her chocolate and then made her way to the keyboard.

"Do you play?" she asked.

"I certainly do. When the pressure is getting too much there's nothing more therapeutic. Music hath charms to soothe and that's why I often pick out *On Top of Old Smoky*. Do *you* want to give us a tune?"

I was surprised at how tentative I was; trying to disguise my nervousness behind daft remarks and unnecessary laughter. But she did agree to play but only on one condition. Of course I asked the obvious question but she said that she would play first and then let me know.

"But doesn't that mean that I will have to agree to the condition?"

She smiled that smile and we both knew she would get her way.

She rattled joyfully through a number of pop standards and then she played *Here Comes the Sun* so beautifully that *On Top Of Old Smoky* curled up in a corner and sulked. When she finished she stood up with a flourish and marched across to me. This was the moment; this was her condition about to be presented. She told me that she had swabbed the decks for the following week: no individual tuition, no school visits and she guessed, quite accurately, that I too could clear a space for a whole week. This was the plan:

"You and I are going to spend seven days in concentrated effort to complete half a dozen songs: tunes, lyrics and arrangements all written and complete."

I began to protest. I did have something on the go about metaphysical poetry and the sermons of John Donne. That was my field after all, not song writing, I couldn't write song lyrics, I told her. But she would have none of it and told me why she was so confident. This is the age of the internet, the age of Google searching and Wikipedia and she knew that I was her man.

"I am?"

"Yes."

She walked right up to me and pressed an impudent forefinger on the tip of my nose.

"Because, when the world begins to ming, you're the man with whom I'd like to sing… Bobby Chime."

Oh joy! Her touch and her just-showered freshness were just an arm's length from me and all around us bells rang. Ringing bells? Ask not for whom they tolled, they tolled for me, my reclusive status and the days of locking myself away. I could feel it in my fingers *and* my toes, there was no hiding place now; the game was up, my cover blown.

Cheshire Life

Steve Dearden

His name was Ian Jebb, hers Susan Hockenhall. David Walsh stabbed Ian Jebb to death inside the Prestbury branch of Williams and Glyns, Susan Hockenhall he took up onto a moor in Staffordshire and left her there to die. It was 1977, I was 17.

If you'd asked then if I'd end up working for a bank … well … all I knew was that I was good with figures, liked people and there was no rush to decide.

David Walsh worked for the company that serviced adding machines, he was 31, he knew Ian Jebb and Susan Hockenhall, knew the branch, boasted about their lax security, he killed Ian Jebb and took two thousand five hundred pounds. They probably didn't have all the warning signs we have now.

BE AWARE STAY SAFE

BEHIND YOU, WATCH OUT FOR TAILGATERS

ASK THE RIGHT QUESTIONS FILL IN THE GAPS

I have been thinking of Ian Jebb and Susan Hockenhall and David Walsh a lot since my daughter moved in with … with him. I don't mean with David Walsh, although he must be around somewhere, he'll have done his twenty-five years now. No, I mean … 'go on say it' that's what my wife says, 'go on say his name.'

I can't.

But I can log in, open his account. Their account.

They've started early today. Online.

07.45 British Airways £12,513.48

07.48 Jumeira 73,429 UAE Diram that's £12,162.68

Another £323.84 would make 10 times £2500. In three minutes. On two of them.

My daughter - I can say her name of course - Anna-Marie. Anna-Marie has moved in with ... him in Prestbury, one of the big houses on the left set back from Castle Hill. In 1977 they were behind hedges up open drives, not the stupid walls and gates they all have now.

I was there in 1977, not in the bank, I went past, on the Wilmslow bus home from school, we slowed down, had a good look at the commotion - a 1977 kind of commotion no stripy tape, no flashing blue lights, no helicopters for police or news, no cameras, no satellite dishes - just the Look North reporter Nick Clarke in his camel coat.

Nick Clarke and a few people standing round with faces so you knew something awful was happening.

My wife says I just have to get my head round it, Anna-Marie has made her choice.

09.15 Woodford Road Service Station, £145. They drive thirsty cars.

My wife fills me in on their news. Their holiday planning, Dubai, the Burj al Arab. She keeps me up to date, how they had to sack their gardener, are going to have to build another extension, how they are ... say it ... say it ... Trying for a child.

Susan Hockenhall and Ian Jebb were engaged, they were 19 and 22, had even set the wedding date I think. I don't know how I found out what happened, whether news had travelled and my Mother told me when I got home, or whether there was something on the radio, a news flash, before news was all the time. What I do know now is the evening story must have been Ian Jebb dead, Susan Hockenhall missing. I have no idea if David Walsh was a suspect in Nick Clarke's report.

Nick Clarke had a good face for bad news, long, lugubrious, heavy lipped. We could use him downstairs in the Crying Room. I am sorry Mrs H, your soon to be ex-husband has frozen your account. I can assure you Mr C, you may think your father was wealthy but all he has left you is debt. No Mr and Mrs L, how your daughter spends her money is her affair, there is nothing I or the bank can do to stop her.

In truth, I have a quiet morning, obviously those were just examples. I can't tell you what my meetings were about or who they were with, or what we discussed. I am a professional. I love this job.

Between times I walk the floor, we have two new girls on meet and greet, good choices, they're fitting in well. Out there in Manchester... him and Anna-Marie spend.

They must be like a force field.

It is not even anyone's birthday.

10.21 Vivienne Westwood £825.00
10.35 Thomas Pink £129.00
11.20 Waterstones £74.98
11.21 Hugo Boss £228.00

12.26 Harvey Nichols £468.48
12.45 Harvey Nichols £575.00

It is not that he is nearly my age that worries me. She has been out with older men before, some of them are still my friends. Some of them even remember 1977. No, I have always liked Anna Marie's boyfriends, whatever age. James. Andy. Ben. Even the actor she went out with until she discovered he was married, Barney he called himself, though his real name was John.

I expect the press said all the things they usually say, how the village would be changed forever by the tragedy. Especially after they found Susan Hockenhall dead. Hypothermia from being out there on a moor in Staffordshire all night, her knees scraped where he dragged her, wrists cut and nails broken trying to free herself, but David Walsh bound her tight. Prestbury didn't change, I doubt if many people still remember the details.

I eat my Havarti cheese and chilli pickle sandwiches in the staff room. My wife insists on making them for me, even though I keep telling her I would happily make them myself. I would reuse the little sealable plastic bag - she uses a new one every day. It's not the money, it's the waste.

I wonder if they are done shopping and have gone home or are having lunch, resting between bouts. I'll soon know.

They must affect the statistics. I said that to them once, You must affect the statistics of wherever you are, a dip in the local economy when you leave. We spent one weekend with them for a wedding near Chester, Anna Marie's best friend from way back, he hired us all a cottage rather than stay in a hotel. Had someone in to cook for us.

Rang in a man from Prestbury to valet his car, a sun roof specialist. He was cold so he nipped out and bought a jumper, and some trousers, and shoes, and ties that happened to be there. The coffee maker jug was cracked, so Anna Marie nipped out and bought one of those silly Clooney machines with the foil discs, we left it in the cottage. He was worried the wedding present wasn't enough, so nipped out to buy a box of champagne from the wine merchants and while he was there a few cases of red for himself... Every time they came back from nipping out they brought bags, not Sainsbury's carriers, I mean paper and cardboard, with fancy logos and crests, string handles. The locals must have thought it was Christmas.

The payment for lunch.

14.30 Manchester House £185.50

More meetings. I imagine myself looking like Nick Clarke. Lower my voice, speak slowly. I am sorry Mr F, we said last time that would be the final loan unless you controlled spending, have you controlled spending? No. So the answer is no, we are closing your account and starting recovery proceedings. This has gone on long enough.

It wasn't that of course, I made that up. Actually I made... a young couple, new business, good.

FILL IN THE GAPS

REMEMBER CLEAR DESK POLICY

They have a clear out the shops policy.

14.44 Oliver Sweeny £195.00

15.50 Hey Little Cupcake £40.00
16.04 Space NK Apothecary £69.00
16.16 Radley £90.00

Then a lull. Afternoon tea? Pre dinner drinks? Staying in town for a show? No. It has gone quiet. In here too, the floor walkers have that chatty-sway way of standing that's nearly home time. And tonight there are drinks upstairs, a birthday.

My wife said I was jealous. Because of his looks. Well you'll have to make your own mind up about that, but I've never looked in a mirror and wished for something different.

She said I was jealous because of his money. I can tell you, you couldn't serve high net worth individuals for twenty years if you envy their wealth. In any case, I grew up with it, not his amount certainly but enough for us, comfortable, I still have my mother's money. More than you'd think. Put away. For a rainy day.

Nick Clarke is dead now, Look North, World at One, Brain of Britain, cancer. Lost his leg.

To reveal details of anyone's account like this is a sackable offence.

Alright, the truth is I didn't like Anna Marie's bloke from the second she introduced him, I didn't like the way he shook my hand, I didn't like the way he looked me in the eye until I had to look away, I didn't like the easy way he had with absolutely everybody, I didn't like his trick of seeming intently interested in everything anybody mentioned, I didn't like the way he held his phone to his head like a slab, I didn't like the way he constantly jiggled his knee.

STAY SAFE BE AWARE

I have to admit that maybe at first I did go looking to confirm my prejudices.

The signs here that say ASK THE RIGHT QUESTIONS FILL IN THE GAPS have words with the letters missing, things like,
F NA C AL C IME
T RR R SM
M N Y L UN ER NG

It was none of those.

The euphemisms on statements may fool wives but bankers recognise the patterns, we know what is going on and where, and how often. Even the cash withdrawals give us leads that usually end up the place we guessed we were going. You can have parallel personal lives, but in the end there is no parallel life for money.

Fill in the gaps.
D UGS
PR ST T TES

Anna Marie and …. and … are home now. Online. Something they forgot.

Hervia £204.

It is time to fall back on my mother's money, the rainy day has come.

There was another character in the Prestbury Williams and Glyn's raid. Police Constable Justin Hardy, 20, son of a judge. Left there overnight to guard the evidence he got bored, wrote jokey ransom notes, £20,000 and the girl goes free chucked them in the bin 25 grand or the girl gets it. In the bin. When David Walsh struck, Ian Jebb and Susan Hockenhall had been sharing lunch. Part of the evidence Justin Hardy was supposed to preserve was a half-eaten sandwich. Justin Hardy ate the sandwich and lost his job. I don't know if he was stupid, or just didn't care. I don't if he loved being a policeman.

Now most people are off home or going upstairs, Jan, Parm, Paula, Jo, Steven, I'll miss them. Family. I collate the evidence, collect the documents in a folder, attach the folder and send to my wife the email that will lose me my job.

It is no defence in banking, an act of love.

The Girl of Lake Silver

Berlie Doherty

This is the story of a girl who fell in love with a fish. But it wasn't an ordinary fish. And she wasn't an ordinary girl. She was a girl who didn't want to grow up.

She lived by a lake in a beautiful valley. Sometimes the lake was busy with boats; yachts with butterfly sails, speedboats with water-skiers towed along behind in white wings of spray; launches full of waving tourists. But at other times the lake was so quiet that she could hear the water breathing, and that was when she loved it best.

When she was very small she used to play on the shores of the lake, paddling and swimming, skimming pebbles to make them bounce across its surface. When her father had finished his work for the day in the hotel kitchens he would take her out in his old rowing boat. What she loved best was to be right out in the very middle of the lake. Then her father would paddle with just one oar so the boat turned slowly round in a circle.

Now she could see how the lake, too, was like a circle. Like a round mirror. The trees on the hillside seemed to turn themselves upside down into it. "The world is under the water!" she laughed. "No," her father said. "What you can see is a reflection of our world."

She understood what he was saying and yet she understood something else too. Deep inside herself she felt that the mirror world of the lake *was* the real world. But she said nothing of this to her father. She didn't tell him how happy she felt when she looked down over the side of the lake and saw her own face reflected there. Her long hair draped down from her shoulders and floated like strands of reeds on the surface. She let her fingertips sip the water, and when she lifted her hand out the water drops slipped away as if they were threads breaking. At times like this she knew that she was part of the water and that the water was part of herself.

"I want to see the world under the water," she would said dreamily.

Her father laughed. She thought how strange it was that grownups didn't understand these things. That was why she didn't want to grow up.

And then, one day, she saw the fish and fell in love with it. Of course, she had seen many fish before. She had seen them leaping for flies on summer evenings. She'd seen them in little silvery shoals, clustered together and flowing through the water in the way that flocks of birds drift through the sky. She had seen the shimmering catch her father brought home sometimes in the bottom of his boat.

One day she went out in the boat on her own. Her mother and father didn't know she had done this and wouldn't have let her go; she knew that. The lake was deep and dangerous. It was so wide that a boat would be lost from sight before it reached the other side. And sometimes, because it was surrounded by mountains, it harboured thunderstorms. She knew all that. And yet when her parents were busy one day in the hotel she took the boat out and rowed as far into the middle of the lake as she dared. She shipped her oars and waited, letting the lake's silence sing to her.

A fish leapt from the water. It flashed with such brilliance that she cried out to it to leap again. But the water was calm except for the ring of ripples the fish had made. They spread out into wider and wider circles until they lapped against the side of the boat, making it rock gently. At last the water settled and lay perfectly still. Yet she could see that there was a glittering circle on the surface of the water where the fish had risen and sunk.

She dipped her oars in and paddled slowly towards the circle, careful not to break it. Now she could see that the circle was made of small bright iridescent flakes like floating stars. And every one of them reflected her face.

Without thinking twice about it she scooped up as many of them as she could and tipped them into the bottom of the boat. There they lay like the tiny pieces of a broken mirror, smiling up at her as she smiled down at them. She wanted to wait and see the fish again, but it was growing dusk and a pink light stole over the water. She must go home.

She moored the boat on the lake shore and gathered up the glittering fragments in her hands. She ran into the cottage near the hotel. "I've found something wonderful!" she shouted. "Come and see! I think they might be stars that have fallen out of the sky." She opened her hand to show her mother, but the jewel flakes had lost all their brightness and had turned dull and brown in her palm.

"Fish scales!" her mother said. "What's wonderful about fish scales? Throw them away, child."

The girl couldn't believe what had happened. But she didn't throw them away. She took them up to her room and threaded them onto a piece of cotton and wore them round her neck all night. But in the morning she hid her necklace inside her dress so no-one would see it and make her throw it away. All she could think about was the beautiful fish, and she longed to row out onto the lake and look for it again, but the chance didn't come. She stood by her window, watching the lake, hoping for a sign of it. For three days it lay like a sheet of white glass.

And then a strange thing happened. Her mother noticed that the girl had shiny flakes like the scales of fish on her arms. "What have you been doing?" she shouted. She bathed her daughter and scrubbed her skin, but nothing she did could remove the scales. She found the necklace, which the girl had hidden under her pillow, and threw it into the lake. "Keep away from that water," she warned her. But the girl couldn't get the leaping, brilliant fish of Lake Silver out of her mind.

Next day, when her parents were both busy she went out in the boat again. As she rowed, the scales on her arms gleamed and flashed in the sun, and she smiled to see them because they were beautiful. She rowed right to the middle of the lake again, where the mountains formed a perfect circle round her and plunged their green arms into the water. She shipped the oars inside the boat and waited. The sun grew cold, clouds gathered in the sky, and still she waited.

She saw many fish leaping for flies, and heard the *plash*! as they sank into the water again. But there was no sign of her mirror fish or the ring of jewels. The light began to grow dim and soft like pearls, and she knew that she should leave. And then, just as the first stars bloomed in the sky, a fish leapt out of the water in a gleaming arc. Everything was reflected in it: the silver speck in the purple sky, the deep blue of the mountain tops, the watery glow of the rising moon. And then the fish sank into the water, leaving a ring of ripples which grew wider and wider and slighter and slighter until all that was left was a circle of floating jewels.

Quickly the girl dipped her oars down and rowed into the circle. She leaned out and saw her face reflected in a hundred different ways in the mirror scales. This time she left them in the water. She knew them for what they were, and she didn't want to drain away their light and their life. But as she looked down at them she could hear the ripple of water all around her, as if it was washing over her, as if she was inside the lake instead of peering into it.

During the night there was a thunder storm. The girl stood at her open window and looked out at the black sky and the lightning forking through it as if it was trying to rip it apart, and she thought of the beautiful mirror fish. She closed her eyes and felt the swish of chopped water around her. She heard the rain drumming above her on the lid of the lake.

"What are you doing, child? You should be in bed." Her mother led her away from the window and pulled back the covers of her bed. Just as the girl climbed in, there was a mighty flash of lightning that lit up the room, and in the white light the mother saw what her daughter had tried to hide from her. Her body gleamed with the scales of a fish. "You must never, never go on the lake again. Do you hear me?" she demanded.

But how could the girl say yes, when every bone in her body ached to be swimming under the black water with her mirror fish?

As soon as her parents were asleep the girl crept out of the house and ran to the lakeside. Her father had filled the boat with rocks, but she had no need of it now. She waded into the lake, up to her ankles, up to her thighs, and when the water lapped against her breasts she knew that she was no longer a child. Joyously she plunged down and down. Reeds stroked her. Little fishes swarmed around her. She turned over and over in her element. The water was like silk streaming across her flesh. In the moonlight she saw how her body gleamed, and how beautiful it was. Her mirror fish swam with her, twisting this way and that, leaping with her into the soft rain.

When morning came, her father and mother stood on the shore of the lake, looking for their daughter. They were frantic with worry. Rain sliced round them like silver arrows. The mountains breathed white mist, and Lake Silver was as grey as ice.

"Our child has gone," the mother cried, and a hush fell across the lake. The mist cleared, the rain stopped. Grey drained away from the sky like smoke and the blue of day poured through. The colours of the mountains reflected green, dun, amber, purple into their own perfect images. There was a holy silence on the water.

The man and woman gazed around them in wonder. They had never known the lake to be so still, or to take the colours of the world into itself so perfectly. Even in their grief for their lost child they wondered at its beauty.

Then they saw the fish leaping into the air. They saw the colours of the mountains and the trees and the sky reflected in it. "How beautiful!" they gasped. The fish made a perfect shimmering arc. As it dipped towards the water the jewel scales fell away from it and there stood their daughter, a young woman in all her beauty. She waded towards them and stood watching with them. The circle of mirror scales spread out around the mother and father and their daughter in a perfect ring, and sank down into the dark, quiet mystery of Lake Silver.

Putting the Fun back in Funeral

Gareth Durasow

> so intimate that your hand upon my chest is my hand,
> so intimate that when I fall asleep it is your eyes that close

Pablo Neruda, Sonnet XVII

The time Rob climbed out of his great-granddad's coffin dressed as his great-granddad was a definite game changer. It was a clumsy setup, hardly worthy of Michael Mann (that's the bloke who directed Heat) but the short of it is that after some japes and capers, Rob ended up lying there in the comfy dark, sweating his nads off, waiting for the moment to strike. I remember thinking during the whole bedlam and the half-arsed police involvement afterwards that this was exactly the kind of thing we'd all be laughing about in years to come. Secretly, I was laughing about it as it happened, but that's because things are always funnier when you're in on the joke – and also a bit pissed.

Even to this day, opinion is divided over this blip in the otherwise flat line that is Rob's family history. I know there's someone out there who sends him a seventy quid bottle of Glenmorangie on the odd birthday and it's always accompanied by a bereavement card. On the other hand, I'm pretty sure that if Rob was on fire right now and Auntie Iredale was standing here holding a glass of water, she would probably think it right and proper to glass him with it. In any case, Rob's debut was the start of something important for Rob.

As for Auntie Iredale, she's a hypocrite; she's been dining off that story for years.

For those in the know about Rob's side enterprise, how he's managed to avoid jail this long is probably a mystery. How he's turned a tidy profit from his public service/blatant sacrilege no doubt gets some people's backs up too – but before you get any ideas, he keeps all his invoices, and his accountant is to the abacus what Christ was to water. The simple truth is that if he's scaring the bejesus out of some funeralgoers, it's because the deceased wanted him to do it. They sign up to it. They want to stick a big middle finger up to all the dreary pomp that their surviving relatives intend to bore the dead fella's mates with. The notable exception being Rob's great-grandad; he had no idea what Rob was planning, but I suppose it's easier to get forgiveness than it is permission – especially when it comes to hijacking someone's last upholstery.

We all know that Rob's been at this for a while but still, I need to choose my next words carefully. With that in mind, our solicitor has advised that I bring your attention to the following:

The subsequent description of Rob's alleged activities over the last few years may seem like a first-hand account, but it is purely speculative. I wish to make no comment at this time about the allegation that I have attended the funerals of those to whom I bear no acquaintance, and with prior knowledge of Rob's planned appearance, nor the allegations that I have been an accessory to the incidents in question. Thank you.

That said, I have it on good authority that it's always spectacular to see him do his thing. There are, however, two occasions that really stand out. I've already glossed over the first because the memories are still a bit raw for some, but that's the one that got the ball rolling, and had it not happened, I dread to think what line of work Rob would have put his creative energies into. Perhaps he'd be surprising some of you with road accident or PPI calls while you're at it hammer and tong with the missus.

The second big occasion is important for a very different reason, and I'd like to share with you what happened, even though from a legal point of view I definitely wasn't there to see it.

You won't survive being Rob's mate for long if you can't appreciate some good-natured irreverence, but what happened at this particular funeral very nearly made me quit my alleged position as Rob's alleged getaway driver.

Watching the lid come off a deceased gentleman's coffin right in the middle of the eulogy and then your best mate climb out never gets old. But when he comes out with a memorised Neruda poem and a ring in a box, it really makes you reconsider your bromance. Public marriage proposals are a bit of a Marmite thing. Personally, I'm more towards the hate side of the spectrum. At best, the bloke knows she's going to say yes and he just wants the whole restaurant, plaza, Eiffel Tower, to see how romantic a specimen of man he is. At worst, he's using the pressure of a spectatorship to compel the poor lass to agree to marry him.

Either way, it's all a bit bleurgh.

The initial reaction to Rob's grand entrance was what you might expect: the sharp gasps; the monosyllabic disbelief; some isolated pockets of restrained outrage; a snort of laughter from someone at the back who'd probably been dying to laugh since the coffin rocked up. Yeah, all that was standard fare, but when Rob missed his cue to leg it and instead cleared his throat to speak, I nearly shat my kegs. The fact that the congregation took it in their stride as best could be expected and didn't rush en masse to string him up from the spire is nothing short of miraculous – truly the house of a wicked God that day – but I honestly believed at the time that the devil would finally catch up with us, and that a portal to the fiery pit was about to open up under my pew and swallow me whole.

Part of me kind of wished for it too.

I'm not sure what I expected him to come out with, but it wasn't the love poetry of a chubby Hispanic bloke. Nearly the whole poem had passed me by before I even figured out what was going on, but my brain caught up just in time to catch the last couple of lines, and they've stuck with me ever since. They're the same lines I recited at the start and I reckon there are plenty of aspiring Casanovas out there who'd rip their right arm off to have come up with them. I would have appreciated the moment a lot more had I been in on the joke at the time – and had I not been bewildered by so many other things, namely: who'd driven Rob to the kind of madness you'd expect from a romantic comedy, if that romantic comedy had been written by someone like David Lynch; why was Billy Idol's White Wedding creeping up in the background; and why wasn't I the one cranking the song up as Rob walked like a boss towards this poor woman sat on the end a few pews back?

In that moment, when he did the unthinkable and actually got down on one knee right next to her, I believed I would have a choice to make: do I pull her off him or do I let her gouge his eyes out with her lady talons?

It was only when she kissed him smack-bang on the lips that I realised how Rob was an enigma even to me. It blindsides you when you find out that you've missed all the stories of your best mate coming to terms with the idea that he's found someone he fancies spending the rest of his life with.

That Rob and Susan spent the whole time afterwards sat next to each other, hand in hand, unmolested, makes me think that there must have been a universal understanding of the bloke everyone was here to pay their respects to; that this was exactly the kind of bonkers spectacle you could expect from any occasion the deceased had some stake in. Like the majority of the room thought, "Oh well, that figures." He was probably the kind of guy who would get wind of his own surprise birthday party and come home early just to play dead in the cellar, and though I never had the pleasure of meeting the man who would have been Rob's father-in-law today, I bet he would have given this young upstart a run for his money, once upon a time.

I often ask Susan if she knew what Rob and her dad were planning, usually when she's had a few, but she's never let on. I like to think that she did know – that she's just as off the chain as her husband. As for keeping me in the dark about the good lady in your life, I see why you did it, Rob. She looks like Gemma Arterton, and you know how I feel about Gemma Arterton. But if she finds that kind of proposal a turn-on, then I think I speak for all the blokes inthe world when I say that we're better off if you take one for the team. We can all sleep a little more soundly knowing that two crazy people are happy together in their crazy world for the rest of their lives.
    Cheers, Rob.

Okay, ladies and gentlemen, I'm aware that I've banged on for ages and that some of you would very much like to forget about Rob's dubious shenanigans and crack on with the buffet. In that case, all that remains to be said is that I'd like you to join me in a toast to the happy couple.
    Susan, I'm sure you know by now what you're letting yourself in for, and that you wouldn't have it any other way. Rob, you're a mad, mad bastard and I love you. May you have a long and happy life together. And remember mate, when it's finally your turn to pop your clogs, I'll be sat in that church with high expectations. Don't let us down.
    And if I snuff it first, you already know what to do.
    Make sure you're there, folks; it'll be something else.

Just hours before he became a saint

Ian McMillan

The man walked down the street, the one he had known since childhood; so much had changed, so much was in the process of decay. Old Mr. Page, the insurance man; Old Mr White, who kept rubber bands in jars marked RUBBER BANDS; Old Mr Marsden, who once gave a scrap man a wheelbarrow and got a threepenny bit for it. Old Mrs Page, who sang as she combed out her long hair; Old Mrs White, who whistled Mr White as though he was a dog. Old Mrs Mardsen, who once gave him a pair of driving gloves. All gone.

He walked to the edge of the street where it folded like a handkerchief in a pocket, and looked out as though he was looking through a window. Across the street there was a dog, a dog like the one that had scared him so much when he was a child that he dare not walk past it to go to school. He waved his hat at the dog to try and frighten it away but the dog stood, dog-still.

A light rain fell, misting his glasses and freckling his face. His friend the artist joined him, stood beside him silently, and as ever the man could think of nothing to say in the face of art. In the face of Art. In the face of ART. Racing pigeons circled overhead, describing something they could not understand but which was about the long rough rope of home. The man and the artist walked.

It was getting dark; a light went on in a house and the man and the artist stared into a room where a woman was watching clouds on a television. The light rain fell. The artist gestured to the gate, and he walked through it with the man. They stood on the lawn in front of the house and watched the woman watching the clouds on the television.

In the room, the woman saw them looking in and recognised them as friends from childhood, from the same class in school, the same pew in church. She gave the man and the artist a cheery wave. There was the sound of a door opening and the closing and the woman came out of the house and stood with the man and the artist and stared with them into the room that she had been in a few moments before. The clouds still moved on the television screen.

The artist spoke: What's that word for moving clouds?
The woman spoke: Scud. Clouds scud.
The man was silent. Of course he knew the word for scud. Of course he was about to say it when the woman said it. If only he'd got in a little more quickly, he could have been the syllable provider. He could have said Scud and the other two would have nodded.
The artist spoke: Not long now. Now long now to when you become a saint.
The woman spoke: Canonisation. That's what they call it. Canonisation.

The man was silent. Overhead, the pigeons circled and the clouds (what's that word?) scudded in the gathering gloom. The artist pointed at the man and said: This time tomorrow you'll be a saint.
The women shook her head and said: I can't quite really believe it. You, a saint. Out of the blue. Right out of the blue.

The rain was getting heavier. The dog came and joined them and the man felt an irritation of fear. The dog looked up at him with utter animal contempt and did not move when a blackbird landed on its head. The dog did not attempt to shake the bird off, but lowered its head towards the man for the man to stroke the bird.
The man whispered: I am not a saint. Stroking the head of the bird would do no good, no good at all. The artist laughed. The woman laughed. It was as though the man had made a joke. The bird stayed on the dog's head.

The man spoke: I'd better be going soon because I've got to go to the ceremony. The actual canonisation.

The artist spoke, making indicating gestures: should we come with you? Me and the woman and the dog and the blackbird? We'd like to come just to see what the ceremony's like.

The silence told the artist quite a lot, and almost as much as he wanted to know. The man shook his head, and said: Only I can be there, only I can witness what becoming a saint really is.

The woman began to sing OOOO in a high keening voice that was almost ululation. The artist joined in, his OOOO blending with hers. The dog sang, his OOOO deep and growly. The blackbird sang, her 0000 leaping from branch to branch. It was almost, but not quite, harmony. It was almost, but not quite, pleasing. The man began to sing, his OOOO soft at first, then getting louder. All the OOOO's became louder and louder, becoming ear-piercing and painful to listen to.

Mr and Mrs Page, Mr and Mrs White, Mr and Mrs Marsden, what would you have made of this singing? What would you have made of the little boy that you knew being on the cusp of canonisation? I hope it would have made you comb your hair and whistle and put rubber bands in a jar and wear some driving gloves and sell insurance and hand over a wheelbarrow, grinning and grinning.

This is how the song went:
OOOOOOOOOOOOOOOOOOOOOOO

Mermaid

Silvia Pio

Mountains rise above the sea and dominate inlets rich in fish and coral. Small beaches shine white among dark rocks, coarse sand made of ancient shells and corals, crumbled and altered by Time. Only pinkish shades reveal the sand's affinity with the submerged structures.

Most of the beaches can't be reached by land as the mountains are steep and deserted, and there has never been any chance or need to build roads.

We used to go there on holidays and weekends. Those trips were a break in the boring working routine and a respite from the summer heat. We would anchor in a creek and each of us would go his or her way, to fish, swim or idle around.

I used to take mask and snorkel and swim away looking for solitude. I liked to spy the coral-coated boulders and cliffs on the bottom of the sea. They were, to me, castles with seaweed gardens and coral bushes, inhabited by a court of vain fish, dressed in crazily bright colours.

One day I happened to dive into a cold current, and had to make for shore to warm up. Just behind a promontory there was a tiny bay. I was sure I had never been there before. I swam towards the shelving beach, the water got shallower and warmer. Now I could stand up and walk to shore. I removed my mask.

She was there. A petite figure sat by the water-line, her feet dipped in the sea. She looked like a little girl. I went closer. How could she have got there? Where could her parents be?

Not aware of me, she was running sand through her fingers and picking out the shells not yet completely polished by the elements. When I was within a few steps, she raised her head and smiled.

She was not a child. She had long hair whitened by the sun and the salty air, a pointed face and sharp features but round eyes. She was wearing a worn out tunic, showing thin tanned arms.

Hello, said I as one always does when meeting somebody in a deserted place, but got no reply. She went on combing sand. I sat down and watched her. Squatting, almost naked, her chin between her legs and hair over her face, she was frenziedly digging the patch of sand in front, as if for buried treasures.

It was time to leave, the others would be waiting for me. I stood up and looked at the sea. As it often happens, the water was stirred by a shoal and some of the fish skipped over the surface scattering flashes of silver as they went.

As at a signal, she rose throwing away all the pieces she had been collecting and like a dart she dived. A splash, a shadow under water, and she was gone. The faint ripples left me with a dream-like feeling. I felt dizzy and couldn't go back to the water. After who knows how long I heard my friends' voices from the boat, relieved to have found me, worried to find me in such state.

On the way back I didn't breathe a word. I never told anyone who, or what, I had seen. But I often went back, trying to find, and never managing to reach, the tiny bay behind the promontory. So I would bend down and look for shells or old coral pieces, in wonder of what treasures they might hide. I'd collect them, threading everything on a string the same colour as the sea. I started wearing the strings around my neck when swimming. I almost drowned once. I started living on a beach and got dark as the mountains around, bleached hair and mad eyes.

Now I live far away from the sea. Here I'm allowed to keep the strings on the bed posts and to pin seaside photos on the headboard. A doctor asked me if there were a place I wanted to go on my annual three-day leave and I replied: to the Mermaid Sea.

Chatterley

Laura Potts

Darling. Your name sleeps hard on my lips. Kiss.

In the candlelight, my lost body over you.
The darkening eyes
        the sly bruise
                the bite.
Night and my dress like a corpse on the floor.
Slower.
    Yes. Deceit.
            More.
My mind does devious things:
Your mouth in my ear
        on my neck then
             down.
                South.

This swelling of lies. Lethal. Nice.

My husband. Ten years away across a table spilling the language
of newspapers, teacups, while the stir of my spoon scalds me to tears.

Look. I waltz out some words: *weathergardensdoctorsbirds*. And outside,
    the mouth of a wind blows our
        filth
under doors. Your claws under clothes.
                            Oh.
Give me a shallot for a long, slow slicing.

Then, I took a walk through the woods where my lips
mimed the memory of kissing, and in my mind,
your laugh was pouring through yesterday's leaves,
the chime of a goblet in the lobes of the trees.
Thieves and we know it, our lust tepid and numb.
The trees are breathing their heavy steam for no-one.
So stay away.
Stay lost.
Stay back.
Keep schtum.

Or down on my knees. Some nights. Whole days chewing tough lies,
   my husband the foul breath of history in my face. Sweet word. *Hate.*
   My marital bed a sour burn, his mouth a foreign place.
     Darling.
He does not know that I, like nobody's child, go to my chamber
and yearn for your limbs; the slim deceit of my bed screaming
             yesyesyesyes;
sucking lies or stirring passion with thin, deliberate spoons.
Watching the moon, I say, to that timeline of centuries clung
to my wedding ring, three words slung across a room
in the cracked blackness of late afternoon to meet you, with
a curdled pond
         made erotic
in my mind, and eyes made sly for no-one but you.

Lover. I weep and remember. Lust
   a thick moan
of a word in the silver purse of my ear,

        on a floor,
           by a door,
  a fierce kiss bruising your lips.
The brush of a night, long as marriage, worn in a bite
on a hard-kissed thigh. The far-off cry of a chanting train
carrying wedding vows, dollies, your name through these walls
in this slither of night. We did it.
          What.
        That.
         Sleep tight.

Or find me a heart that is blacker than mine. There are wires
in my veins I could throttle with, snakes spitting lies in the rope
of my spine. Time
        a slow
               plunging
                       of bodies,
              sprawling
                      and slurred,
   the taste of a curse
          that is sound
                and not word.
Then biting awake to a clatter of plates
with my husband, years ago, talking birds.

But.
On the other side of this night, like twenty years
in the distance between us, the wind turns his mouth to the house
    and rises,
           his loins clumsy,
                    his eyes dumb,

come to the candle - a sputtering actor, a stammering tongue -
come to
        that bed
                with its hard-punctured lung
that remembers me, where hung on the ceiling
  is the chiming of bells -
    the bells of my breasts -
        the globes of your buttocks,
    faster, *yes,*

where the dress on the floor, bared of its bones, moans out
its four hundredth winter. Time slows. A splintering woodland
that hardens its heart sleeps in some part of a long-smudged
childhood where pealing of voices tolls out the years.
    The taste of a word
        on a tongue
          in an ear.
Go light some candles. Rip me up. Here.

Darling. You burn and I simmer. Long nights
in criminal sheets,
    the bow of my body,
        the slow vestal shriek
of unlit flames that pearl for your skin.
The slipping of shadows, silver and thin,
in the hall, by a wall, the long-swallowed lies
spilling out with a
      bite,
        the dregs of an evening,
         a long-shaken
night.

Then sometimes,
by a fireplace,
    I see the plush of your hands
        and chink of your cheek
weak in the hinge of a sweet, rotten heart where part
of a woman, a ghost in a bed, slips through the lips
       of a long-kissed dress.
Dead.
    Once held in your hand, locked in a lung.
Then laid on a floor. Signed by your tongue.

You make me do this.
    Now.
My heart ripped out like the tongue of a tide.
    Cawed.
           Lied.
                    Cried
for your hands, for the slither of touch,
    your mouth on my breasts,
  the smudge
  and the sketch
of two lovers in lamplight.
                Just once.
                        Sex.

    Up a wall.
        Faster.
  We did it.
        Didn't we.
                Yes.

And you'll do it again. *A child come calling to Chatterley's bed,*

said with a groan
                in the long,
                                      distant
                  moan
of that floorboard
  that whines
        with our festering lies
see the bones of a lover
     a mother
         a wife
the passionate hands of the clock as he waves past
the time to my spine on the cold cobalt floor
     the curve of my back on the skin of the door
        the snap of the jaw and
                     the lash
                         of the tongue
   the gold of your ribcage
             the silver of lung

Done. In the corner, you pull on your shirt. The hurt of your heart swells in the firelight, spills into the air between us. No words. Locked throats.

I feel ten years from you.

Hand me my coat.

The Miller's Tale

Richard Smyth

It is difficult to say or write the words.

Ignaz Brno-Hálavyí is dead.

Perhaps only those of you who are fortunate enough to be Hungarian will know him. Perhaps, even, only those of you who have seen the black chimneys of Eöstvöt and breathed the city's bitter air. Perhaps only those who have visited the terraced grey-brick house on Mogyoró Street in which Brno-Hálavyí was born and died.

Or it may be that, after all, none of us truly knew him.

But we know his work.

Or perhaps, in fact, we do *not* know his work.

Ignaz Brno-Hálavyí came into the world in December 1912. As a boy, he was fascinated by nature, by the world around him. He would spend hours foraging in the storm-gutters for drowned birds. His father, an engineer, would bring him home curious rocks, brightly coloured pebbles, chunks of rare minerals. 'You must be careful with those, little Ignaz,' his father would say to the inquisitive boy, 'for, if you lose them, I will give you a good hiding.'

There were few other children living in industrial Eöstvöt at that time. Ignaz was schooled at the home of Father Florian, a retired Orthodox priest who taught him to recite 'The Story of Prince Árgirus' in Greek and beat him with a length of hose. Ignaz was a good scholar. He was resilient. He endured. Happiness would find him.

Eva Selymes was the dark-eyed daughter of a soap merchant. When Ignaz met her in nineteen thirty-one, she was seventeen, a budding actress, beautiful in spite of her lame left leg, the flower of the Eöstvöt stage. Ignaz – a shy big-nosed boy shivering nightly at the stage-door – courted her with glazed pastries and poems he copied from books.

It is known that for many years they exchanged letters. This is all that is known. In nineteen thirty-seven, Selymes the soap-merchant discovered Ignaz's letters tied with a ribbon beneath Eva's bed. He flushed them into the city sewer, and forbade her to write again to her big-nosed lover. In nineteen thirty-nine, Eva died from water-borne cholera. Ignaz burned her letters.

In nineteen forty-five, with the artillery of the Third Ukrainian Front darkening the skies over Eöstvöt, Ignaz, in the candlelit loft of his parents' home, took up a pen, unscrewed the cap from a bottle of ink, spread a sheet of white foolscap upon a desktop, and began to write.

Why does the writer write? As well ask why the fire burns, why the wheel turns, why time goes by.

Az Ókory. 'The Ancient'. Ignaz Brno-Hálavyí's greatest novel. Of such a book, what can a man say.

Miklós Bánat – the name would translate as 'Grief', if anyone were to translate it – is a miller's apprentice in the fictional Hungarian village of Nógrád. When Miklós is a boy, his father, a cruel, proud man, is killed in a mining accident. To support his mother, Miklós must work hard at the mill. He grows bent-backed from the labour and wheezy from the dust. The flour turns his black hair white. The miller – a kindly soul – takes pity: you are a young man, Miklós, he says, and yet you stoop and cough like an ancient. I have heard what the boys in the village call you. *No*, cries Miklós. Yes: *Nagypapa Miklós* they call you, nods the miller. 'Grandpa Miklós'.

You will mill no more, Miklós, says the miller. I will sell my flour to you cheaply, and you will be a baker. So Miklós becomes a baker. He grows to be a man. His back straightens, he no longer coughs, he combs out the flour from his hair. He marries a beautiful lame girl whom he woos with glazed pastries. And then, when the trumpet sounds, he goes to war.

He fights, Miklós, at Mărăști, and Doberdó, and Komarów, and he fights with valour, though he loses an eye at Doberdó. But in the war Miklós sees only futility and woe. Over the battlefield he grieves; in the dressing-stations and field hospitals he mourns. And though he is gone only a year he returns to Nógrád an old man once again. His beautiful wife does not know him, and when he tries to explain, she laughs, and calls him *hunchback*, and *knock-knee*, and *white-beard*. She goes off to marry a wealthy engineer. And the townspeople point at Miklós in the street and call out: *Nagypapa Miklós*.

Miklós, for all his wisdom, is friendless, and weeps. Winter comes to Nógrád. The snow falls. And the novel ends.

And now I, Miklós Bánat, Miklós the miller's apprentice, Miklós the baker, Miklós the soldier, *Nagypapa Miklós*, one-eyed Michael Grief, stand before you and say: Ignaz Brno-Hálavyí is dead.

Perhaps you don't know him. Even if you are a Hungarian, even if you did visit black-chimneyed Eöstvöt, even if you called for black tea or a glass of *pálinka* at the little house on Mogyoró Street, you wouldn't have known him. And would you have known the work, 'The Ancient', *Az Ókory*, Ignaz's greatest novel? Would you the blazes. It was never translated into English. What's more, it was never published in Hungarian. And for why? Simply because it was no damned good. It was declined by seven publishers and now it sits tied with string in the loft of the house of Ignaz Brno-Hálavyí's long-dead parents.

Who mourns its author? *I* mourn him.

It was not a good book. Ignaz was not a good writer, he had no gift. Look at me, for instance: I am a thin character, very thin. Tiresome, also. And my wife? Barely plausible. You should hear our dialogue. It is stilted and unrealistic.

My opinions are trite and misguided. My emotions are sentimental. In chapter fifty-eight Ignaz forgets which of my eyes is missing. I should cry, with the monster made by Frankenstein, 'Accursed creator! Hateful day when I received life!'.

But I do not. I stand here in mourning, and my mourning is sincere. Ignaz Brno-Hálavyí made a man. Let people say that, if they have nothing else to say. Ignaz made *me*. So though he made no money (he worked all his life in an Eöstvöt steel mill), and though he loved no woman (save one, in vain), and though his book is *the most awful swill* (so said the gentleman at Kolszvar and Son) –

Let it be said, if nothing else be said, that he lived a long life, and that he made a man. And that for god's sake he *was* a man. Even though now he swings from a rope knotted around a roofbeam. Even so, let these things be said.

Excerpt from Storybank: The Milkfarm Years

Jane Steele

PROLOGUE

If I thought anything within these pages was remotely implausible, I would ask you to suspend your disbelief.

In the world I depict history – or as it's now termed "hystery" – is not just written by the winners, though such a renaming will give you a generous clue as to who the winners are. It is simply written, by whoever feels like it, with the apparent democracy of an even more developed information age.

This is not a story about the failure of female power. On the contrary, it was imperative that women took full charge. It happened as if by osmosis: peacefully, bloodlessly and rightly. It was also a matter of necessity. Before and after the events depicted here, women governed wisely and well....

...

Perhaps the best way to begin would be to include the following sad, rambling, badly-punctuated little note. It speaks volumes of how things had become. For young men such notes were, sadly, as common as colds.

Entry One
Handwritten, bloodstained.
Eliot Pickavance-Jones – Suicide Note
Dear Mum and Dad

   I will be dead very soon but before I go I want to explain why. Not that I owe you anything never mind an explanation but you know what I mean.

   It's frustrating to die with so many questions on my mind that I know now will never be answered.

I want to know why as family we all acted in the way we did that made me the way I am that made me do this. Ask yourselves after I'm gone.

I want to know why none of us could look the truth in the face.

I want to know why we lied to each other so completely when we were supposed to love each other.

When I was going to that therapist –we decided together (despite what you might think he was NOT brainwashing me, Father!) that I'd grown up thinking love was lies.

I didn't want to talk about the weather. I wanted to talk about why I felt so lonely sad confused and scared all the time. We didn't do that so I never learnt how so here I am in this situation. It's your fault.

Look after Tarquin for me. I wish, I REALLY wish I could have been the "big brother" he needs and deserves. Leaving him behind pains me more than anything seeing as I've GIVEN UP COMPLETELY on you two and YOU WILL NOT BE MISSED. The logical thing to do would be to take him with me, but how can I when I'm stuck in here and you won't let me see him anymore?

So what I want to say is, look after him for me. If you can. And that's a big if, because look what you've done to me!! If you can't, then open your mouths FOR ONCE and ask someone who can. Do him – and me – that one service. I won't call it a favour. You should have done it for me and you DIDN'T.

I've managed to get hold of a glass. Silly people. Now I've got the equipment, it's time. Goodbye.

Entry Two.
Draft paper transcript of audio bug.
** ILLEGAL DUMP**. No traceable source.

<u>ABOVE TOP SECRET</u>
<u>DRAFT minutes of Special Projects cabinet sub-committee meeting</u>

'Operation Rocking Horse'
4.06 a.m. 17th June 2321.
Thora Hird House, Ripon, England

Present:
First Minister: Juno Kimson
Home Secretary: Aurelia Maude
Business Secretary: Sandra Thorne
Minster for Gender Affairs: Carmel Kevinson
Minister for the Environment: Nuada Patrick
Attorney General: Martina Woolf
Chancellor of the Exchequer: Amira Khan-Smith
[Minute taker: Tarquin Irrelevance Pickavance-Jones]

Apologies
Chief Medical Officer: - Heather Anndaughter.

Juno Kimson ("JK"):- Right, we know what we're here to discuss. Let's get on with it quickly, I have four other meetings today...
Sandra Thorne ("ST"): Juno, this is an important subject, we can't rush on any discussions. I'm not going to be bulldozed on this one.
JK: We've been talking for months, we need to finish talking.
ST: Clearly not, otherwise we wouldn't be sitting here doing it again.
Nuada Patrick ['NP']: Is Claire on her way?
JK: I've heard from her. She's going to be late, she has to get back from holiday and then get herself here.
Martina Woolf ("MW"): Have we got a chair for this meeting?

Silence.

JK: (signing) I suppose it's me again, then. Don't cocking well moan and say you're not given the chance. We always have this rigmarole; I keep offering to rotate it…

Cries of "all right" and "yeah, yeah".

Hush! Now, the issue at hand is serious.

NP: It's been allowed to become serious. If we'd acted earlier, we could have done something about it. I am SURE there are other ways of handling this.

Carmel Kevinson ['CK']: I don't think the time would have made any difference and in terms of action I don't think we have a choice. We've got the survival of the bloody country in our hands here…

NP: We don't have a choice? We run the show, for crying out loud! If we don't have a choice, who does?

Amira Khan-Smith ("AKS"): Carmel, don't try and back the rest of us into a corner. Have you any idea how much this is going to cost?

CK: Are you boiling this down to transfers again, Amira? Just make some bloody more, however you do it. We can't worry about the cost when we've got this shitpile on the table. We have to ensure the survival of the people.

AKS: You're trying to justify what you see as a foregone conclusion when there are diverse views…

[Several voices start to speak at once].

Aurelia Maude: ("AM"): THE QUESTION, OF COURSE… ladies, please!

ST: Ladies?? What is this – the Pale Ages?

JK: Sandra! Everyone!

[Silence].

AM: Thank you - that's better! The question is how we are going to do this and that's what we're here to finalise today, and I must emphasise the word finalise. We simply cannot prevaricate any longer.

JK: Thank you, Aurelia. The voice of reason, as per usual, though I must add that I'm certain none of us are prevaricating, we have simply fully explored all the options.

AM: Of course, Juno. My apologies.

JK: Accepted. I think the central question is how to bring them in with the minimum of fuss.

MW: By 'with the minimum of fuss' you mean 'under the radar'.

JK: I mean with the minimum of fuss. This is a hugely emotive issue. We don't want recycling capsules going through shop fronts en masse, it's just not necessary if we do it in the right way and my thoughts on the right way are perfectly clear and have been for some time.

MW: So these talking shops have simply been an exercise, have they?

JK: Martina, I don't mean to be absolutist but I respectfully remind you that I am the First Minister. It will be my signature on the bill...

MW: And mine.

JK: [slight pause] Please remember who is ultimately responsible here. I can't help but feel passionate about this. We all have to steer it to a conclusion. Please bear in mind our respective roles in this.

MW: You're pulling rank.

JK: I am NOT pulling rank. How else are we to get this done unless the cocking First Minster does her job? It's not about pulling rank!

AM: Juno's right, Martina. We need to crack on. Do we have any sort of agenda?

ST: No, it's all too bloody last-minute. Flaming Nora! We're trying to decide whether to bring this thing in nationwide and we can't even run a meeting of half a dozen.

MW: Seven. There's seven of us if you don't count the boy.

ST: Six, seven, whatever. You know what I mean.

AKS: It's a good job you're not the cocking Chancellor, Sandra!

(Laughter)

JK: (sound of clicking fingers) You. Typist. What's your name....?
Tarquin Pickavance-Jones ['TPJ']: Tarquin.
JK: Speak up, I can't hear you!
TPJ: TARQUIN.
JK: Tarquin, was there any agenda circulated before this meeting? I can't remember if I asked for one to be prepared.
TPJ: I don't know, Mistress. Not as far as I'm aware.
ST: It's pointless asking him, he looks like he's shitting himself as it is. Are you new, lovie? Never mind, you'll get used to us. Think on: don't take down ANYTHING conversational or remotely off-the-record sounding, all right? Just policy and procedure. If in doubt, just put "discussed". Let's crack on, sistren.

Elephant Gin

Michael Stewart

The poster on the door says: 'It's gin o'clock'. You clasp the handle. This is your sixth blind date since she left you, but it hasn't got any easier. Like going for an interview for an important job: there is an anxious toad squatting in your gut. The door opens into a small room with mismatched tables and chairs and a bar front with lots of different gins behind it. You look around and you see her sitting on her own in the corner. She looks both different and the same as her photograph. Her name is Melanie.

Isn't all gin more or less the same? you ask after you've said hello and sat down at her table.

There's gin and there's gin, she says. Then there's all the things you add. Different garnishes.

How do you mean?

That one has a slice of orange. You get a sprig of rosemary with that one. This one comes with different berries. They just put a bit of pepper in that one, she says as she points at gins on the menu she's holding.

You look at your date as she talks about gin. About your age, early thirties, with short straight hair that's dyed a rich mahogany. Her eyes are grey. Her nails are painted army green. She has a tattoo on her wrist but you can't tell what it is without making it obvious that you're staring. You think about asking her but it feels too personal this early into the date. Even though it's on public display. She hadn't mentioned it on her profile. They usually do. You look around the room. A few arty types. Men with hipster beards. Women wearing glasses they don't need to wear. You thought you'd get better at it with practice. Dating. It's been nearly a year since Louise left you.

You spent over an hour getting ready, as you always do. Checking for nasal hair, whitening your teeth. You gave yourself a good talking to: you can do it. You're interesting. You're smart. You're reasonably good looking. No obvious abnormalities, apart from a scar on your arm from when you had chicken pox. Then you whitened your teeth again and changed your shirt into something with a plainer pattern.

There was Emma. She was the first after Louise. A bit of an Amy Winehouse beehive and a laugh like Sid James. You'd gotten on at first. Tried out a few bars. Had some tapas. On the third date she'd invited you back to her place. She was self-conscious about a mastectomy she'd had two years ago and switched the lights off. You'd stroked the scar above her heart and felt her flinch. Afterwards she had wanted to plan the next three dates. She had some mates in a rockabilly band. Did you want to go and see them?

She thought it was funny that you didn't have a diary. How do you remember dates? I just do, you'd said. A few days later a parcel came through the post. It was a calendar and she'd written in the days you were going to be seeing each other. There was a six-month anniversary, and even a holiday together in the summer. She'd drawn a cartoon of you on a beach throwing a ball. You ignored all her phone calls and texts. Eventually she stopped contacting you.

Then there was Karen who loved your cock. She told you every day how much she loved your cock. Until you started thinking that there was something wrong with your cock. It was just a cock, wasn't it? No one had ever mentioned it before. Not especially big. Not especially small. Just a normal, average cock. But she'd gone on about it so much that in the end you became self-conscious. And then you couldn't perform. It's ok, she'd said. It happens. But it had never happened before. And when you stopped ringing her she didn't ring back.

After that was Yvonne. She had five children and given birth to them all at home. They didn't go to school. She could educate them better herself, she said. School education wasn't education, it was brainwashing. She was still breast feeding her youngest, even though he was six.

I've got a cat, Melanie says.

You nod.

Are you ok with cats?

You shrug.

Some people don't like them. Or they're allergic.

I'm not allergic to cats, you say.

She smiles, good. I'm glad. I don't like men who don't like cats.

It's not that you dislike cats, it's just that you don't like pets in general. You wouldn't want to see them suffering, but you don't usually bond with them. Keen to change the subject, you ask her how her day has been.

Mad at the moment. She takes a berry out of her glass and places it on her tongue. We're trying to get funds for a new project.

What's the project? You ask.

It's a community venture called Green Futures. It's an engagement and impact project.

You nod, as though you understand.

It's about sustainability. And bringing disparate elements of a community together. Challenging stereotypes.

I see, you say.

You stare at her tattoo again. It swirls and curves and folds in on itself.

What do you think of the gin? She asks.

Nice.

You are drinking elephant gin, on her advice. She tells you about all the different botanical ingredients. Lion's tale and devil's claw. Wormwood and ginger. It just tastes like gin to you.

Try mine, she says, and offers you her glass. You take a sip.

It's Monkey 47. It's from the Black Forest. What do you think?

Nice, you say. But you can't tell the difference between the two gins.

Has this place been open long? I've never noticed it before.

About a year. But they don't advertise. It's all word of mouth. I like it because it's right in the centre of town, but it never gets too busy. You could be anywhere. It doesn't feel like a town bar. Drink up, she says. I want you to try another.

Outside the sky is black and the air has cooled. You pull up the collar of your jacket. She holds onto your arm. You wander up a snicket.

So what do you want to do? You ask. Do you want another drink or do you want to get something to eat?

Let's go back to mine, she says, and gives your arm a squeeze. She flags down a black cab.

You climb into the back and she sits next to you, pressing her body against yours.

You sure you're ok with cats? She asks again.

Absolutely.

He's a bit of a pest, to be honest. He doesn't mean to be, but he can be a bit clingy. And he gets jealous. He's lived with me a long time. I guess he feels protective. It's good to have him there though. I feel safer when he's around.

The taxi pulls up outside a Victorian terraced house. You reach into your pocket and root around for some money. But she's got her purse out and she's handing the driver a twenty.

Keep the change, she says, and grabs your arm.

This is great, you tell yourself. Try and relax. Enjoy it. A beautiful, intelligent woman, wants you to come back to her house. You're a lucky man, you tell yourself, and you try and fight away the waves of doubt. The house has three floors that stretch above you.

She finds her key and unlocks the door. She takes you by the hand and leads you into the kitchen. There's a breakfast bar and a bread machine.

Do you want another drink? She says.

I'll have whatever you're having.

I fancy some vodka. How about a vodka martini?

She mixes the drinks and takes out some olives from the fridge. You sit at the kitchen table opposite her. She takes off her shoes and runs her foot down your leg. You try not to show your nervousness.

I like you, she says. You don't say a lot, but I don't mind. There are different kinds of silences, don't you think? You know, sometimes it's uncomfortable being with someone if they're quiet, but you're not like that.

Where's the cat? You ask, as you look around the room.

He must be out, she says. Don't worry about the cat. He can look after himself. Shall we go to bed?

In her bedroom she lights some candles and undresses. You stand there watching, not sure what to do. You put your drink down by the bed and go over to her. You embrace her naked body. Her skin is smooth and you trace her curves with your fingers. Her lips and tongue taste of vodka and vermouth.

Take your clothes off, she says, breaking away from your embrace. She climbs into bed and pulls the covers up to her chest.

You feel foolish as you fumble with your buttons. You place your jacket over the back of a chair and undo your shirt. You want to fold it, but think this is too formal, so you throw it over the jacket. Next your shoes. You don't bother to unlace them. You just flick them off at the heels. You bend down and peel off your socks. You unzip your trousers and let them fall to the floor. You step out of them.

And your underpants, she says, get them off.

You blush a little, but do as you are told. You cup your cock and balls and edge towards the other side of the bed. She giggles as she pulls back the covers for you.

Jump in, she says. Don't be shy.

She climbs on top of you and kisses your face, your neck, your chest. You feel her hair on your skin. You feel her warmth and her softness. Then you hear the back door open.

What's that? you ask.

Don't worry, it's just the cat.

How can the cat have opened the door itself? You think, but maybe it wasn't closed properly to begin with. You stroke her hair and cup one of her breasts. She kisses you hard on the lips and probes with her tongue. It feels like a snake in your mouth. Your hands wander over her body, along the curve of her hips and over her buttocks. You take one in your hand and squeeze the flesh. There's a scratch at the door.

What's that? You ask.

It's just the cat, ignore him. He'll go away if we ignore him.

You kiss again and take her in your arms. You turn her round, so that now you are on top and she is underneath. You kiss her neck and her shoulders. You kiss her breasts and take a nipple in your mouth. It's big and hard. She's got hold of you, and she's guiding you in. There's another scratch at the door, this one more insistent.

I'll have to let him in, she says. It's a cold night. You don't mind, do you?

You shrug.

She gets up and goes to the door. She opens it and then jumps back into bed. You stare at the figure in the doorway. It's not a cat. It's a man. Of average height and build. He wears blue overalls and a red baseball cap. He shuffles into the room and closes the door. He shuffles over to the bed and stands next to it.

You don't quite know how to react. Who's this? You ask at last.

This is the cat.

But-

You don't mind do you? He's no trouble really.

I-

You'll forget he's here in a minute.

She reaches across to you and strokes your arm. She leans in to kiss you but all you can see is the man in blue overalls and red baseball cap, standing over you. You pull away.

What's the matter? She asks.

I can't, you say. I've got to get back.

Come on, don't be silly. Come here. She puts her arms around you and pulls you closer to her. She kisses you on the cheek.

You're tense, she says. How about I give you a massage?

She starts to rub your shoulders and your neck, and you feel yourself relax.

Can I get in with you? It's the man she calls the cat.

Not now, she says. Can't you see I'm busy?

But I'm cold.

No.

She digs her thumbs into the muscles below your collar bone and the pain you feel is good.

Please.

Not now.

I won't wiggle.

Yes you will.

They start to bicker. You try to ignore the growing argument between the woman and the man the woman calls a cat, but you can't. Instead, you get out of bed and get dressed.

I'm going, you say.

Look what you've done now? She says to the cat.

She looks at you imploringly. The cat just stares at his feet. He has no shoes and socks on.

I'll give you a call, you say, fastening your jacket.

You always have to spoil it, don't you? You can't stand seeing me happy, can you? You SELFISH FUCKING CUNT!

You close the door behind you and leave the house.

It's still dark outside. You flag down a cab and give the driver your address. When you get home you will have a glass of warm milk and watch a documentary about the Industrial Revolution.

The fellow from whom came the sea

Matthew Hedley Stoppard

Old accusations throbbed inside the Teacher's head but he kept trampling across the field in the afternoon heat. Clumps of dry soil crunched and crumbled under his brogues. A sweltering jacket made the shadows under his armpits darken his shirt. Unbuttoning his collar released steam from his torso and sweat dripped from his nose and upper lip. A hidden furrow flung him into the Boy at his side.

Ugly aerials and satellite dishes came into view where the farmland ended and the Teacher was reminded of what happened in a Devonshire suburb two years ago. He nudged the Boy:

"Are you sure Peter wants to see me? Isn't he too ill for visitors?"

"Definite, sir. He likes them stories you tell about livin' next tuh sea, where you're from."

The Teacher sneered at the Boy's rumpled appearance; the dirty fingernails and greasy black hair that looked like starling feathers. But Peter was a star pupil: studious and obedient with good attendance – until he fell ill.

A tussock collapsed under the Teacher's foot and he tumbled again.

"Isn't there another way to Peter's house?"

"It's a flat, sir"

"You know what I mean. Is there a different route?"

"Yeah, but this is quickest, sir. Any road, you can see it now."

There was a eggshell-coloured tower block up ahead.

Clouds covered the sun and a breeze crept up the Teacher's sleeve, cooling the air beneath his clothes. He thought about Torquay and balked.

"I think I should go back to school. Peter can wait for another time to hear some stories…"

The Boy panicked and tugged the Teacher's arm.

"No, sir. It's gotta be now. We're nearly there. He really wants to hear about the sea."

"Really?"

"About the mermaids, sir. *And* the pirates with funny beards. Seahorses, Noah and the whale…"

"*Jonah* and the whale. It's *Noah* and the Ark."

"…Noah and the Ark, giant squids, submarines, the Titanic and Homer and the police sirens."

"Police sirens?"

"On the rocks, sir. Singing to the sailors, hypnotising 'em."

"Oh, I see. They're just called sirens; they entice Odysseus and his crew on their way back home to Ithaca."

"Definite, sir. Come on."

Peter and the other children watched the Teacher and the Boy approach the tower block. They sniggered at his flapping gait, wading through loose soil in hard shoes and a heavy suit. Someone brought out more water balloons and put them with the others wobbling on the balcony.

All apprehension left the Teacher's mind. Stepping onto tarmac, the Boy pointed to the intercom and told him Peter's flat number. The Teacher straightened himself and slid his tie knot to his Adam's apple in case there were parents to meet.

He had memorised *The Rime Of The Ancient Mariner*, parts one to three, for tomorrow's lesson but would recite it for Peter should he miss more school.

The Teacher raised his hand to press the buzzer when the Boy ran off, shouting: "Now!" Suddenly wild-eyed infant faces appeared on all the first floor balconies.

A water balloon exploded on the Teacher's shoulder. He looked up to see Peter jumping up and down, fists clenched, shouting: "Paedo! Paedo! Paedo!"

Staggering backwards the Teacher looked around him and stood helplessly as a barrage of multicoloured bombs descended upon him, soaking him to his core, accompanied by more chants of "Paedo! Paedo! Paedo!"

Surly adults came to their doorways to stare. And nothing else.

The Teacher was drenched in his shady reputation. He pictured Peter, behind a banister, eavesdropping on his parents' whispered conversations. How a rumour had followed him to another county.

He squelched back home to call the headmaster, and went to bed leaving a trail of muddy footprints behind him.

Welcome to Horbury

William Thirsk-Gaskill

I am living in a posh part of Leeds, and splitting up with my wife. That might sound bad, but the break-up is nothing compared to the marriage that preceded it. I am feeling pretty good. I sleep on an air-mattress, downstairs, in the front room.

'I know we are getting divorced, but you don't have to sleep down here,' she says, one of the first few nights. Yes, I do.

The divorce will cost me a mere six-hundred and ninety-five pounds. Once we agree we are going to do it, there is no dispute about money, or anything. It is the only harmonious thing we ever do.

I join a couple of online dating agencies. My ex-wife-to-be stalks me in one of them, but that's another story.

In the other one, without any stalking, I meet Lois. Lois lives in Wakefield. She has a 7 year-old son. She is also in the midst of getting divorced. Her estranged husband has defaulted on the mortgage on the family home, and she and her son are about to be evicted. She is studying for a degree, which she wants to complete.

This dating site has the facility to set questions next to your profile. The default questions are all clichéd nonsense. I write my own.
1. If we were going out for the evening, and I said, "Tonight, money is no object," would that bother you?
2. Do you know what it says on the front of your passport?
3. If, after a while when we had not said anything to each other, I took hold of both your hands, and looked into your eyes, would you think it was weird?
4. If we were sitting down to dinner, and the phone rang, would you answer it?
5. Do you ever read books by authors who died more than 50 years ago?

Lois gets 4 out of 5.

We exchange contact details, and I start sending her text messages. I want to meet her. She keeps telling me that things are too complicated for her to be able to see me. But she put her profile on a dating site, and she answered my questionnaire. Hers are the only set of answers worth having. The other two are from obvious nutters.

We have lovely, long text conversations. Only one of them goes wrong. My estranged wife comes in, and I have agreed (we are still living under the same roof) to cook dinner for both of us. I text Lois to say that I have to get back to cooking dinner for the estranged wife. Lois misinterprets this to mean that I am still entangled in my failed marriage. 'Goodnight! I don't want to play second fiddle.' I manage to talk my way out of it, using the very same skills that I want to abandon, once my divorce has gone through. Things are kind of all right.

We talk on the phone. I suggest that we spend the night at a hotel in Leeds, and that I will pick her up. I have to find an address in a place called Middlestown. Middlestown turns out to be in the middle of frigging nowhere, in semi-rural South West Yorkshire. I have to slow down twice for horses. That is after we resolve the confusion between pubs called 'The Bull's Head', 'The Black Bull', and 'The Little Bull'.
    We make it to the hotel. We have dinner. Lois appreciates the soup. She says it is the nicest soup she has ever tasted.

My therapist has told me that it is a wise move to meet a potential new partner on the neutral ground of a hotel.

Lois asks me to come to her house, the rented house in Horbury she has moved into after the repossession, to meet Liam, her 7 year-old son. We both agree that Liam's opinion of me will be decisive, regarding the future of our relationship.

Liam has a remotely-controlled, dancing robot, which doesn't work. I inspect it. Liam and Lois keep asking me how I am doing, during the inspection. I ignore them. I find a set of double-A batteries in the body of the robot, which I replace. I replace the triple-A batteries in the remote control. I pronounce a Native American, shamanistic benediction upon the robot, and its remote control. I switch both units on. I press a button on the remote control. The robot shakes its hips. The phone rings. Lois answers, hands the phone to Liam, who explains to his biological father how delighted he is that I have got the robot working.

I start referring to the two of them, Lois and Liam, as The Ells.

I go to the 3 for 2 table in the children's department of Waterstones, in Leeds. I see nothing that I recognise. I leave the shop with a set of books about a character called Mr Gum. I wonder if they will be enough.

On the way back to Wakefield, I stop at Toys R Us in Cathedral retail park, and buy a plastic model of the Millennium Falcon, which costs over a hundred pounds. At least, if you stand the box on its end, it is about the same height as Liam.

A few days later, I have finished reading the promised three chapters of 'You're A Bad Man, Mr Gum,' to Liam, before he goes to bed. Liam declares that I am, 'miles better' at reading stories than Lois, at which Lois looks annoyed. I shut the book. Liam is still wide awake.
    'One more chapter,' says Liam.

'No. We said three chapters. You've had three chapters. It is time for bed, now.'

'One more chapter,' says Liam.

I decide that I will read one more chapter, especially because I am enjoying the story, and Lois seems to approve of the way that Liam is engrossed in it.

'One more chapter,' I declare. 'One more chapter, and then it is time for bed. Is that agreed?'

Liam nods.

I turn the page.

'Chapter Four. Mr Gum Has A Cup Of Tea.'

Liam looks attentive. I read the text of the chapter. It is one sentence. 'Mr Gum had a cup of tea.' That is all there is. That's all he gets: a title, and then a change of tense.

Liam demands to inspect the book. He accuses me of having known in advance what Chapter Four was like, which is utterly without foundation. He gets taken to bed, anyway. It is almost certainly the first time in Liam's life that he has heard someone say the word, 'calumny'.

Later, in the same series, we come across the word, 'zamzastical'.

'What does zamzastical mean?' asks Liam.

'I think it can mean anything you want it to mean.'

'Can it mean, "gay boy"?'

My house in Leeds is so full of junk that I have no idea of how to market the property, but Lois helps me. After about another year, that house is sold, and the three of us move in together, in Horbury.

The kitchen is tiny, and the bathroom is antiquated. We engage a builder to construct an extension.

It is a big project. For at least a month, we have no cooker, and no bathroom. We move into a nearby hotel.

Once all the major work is complete: the new roof, the building of the extension, all the plastering, electrical work, the new floors, and plumbing, I run out of money. I have to call a halt to the project. Lois complains that the newly-built rooms smell of damp dog, and so I paint some of them, myself, starting with the bathroom, to cover up the bare plaster. We argue for a while about what causes the smell of damp dog. Eventually, it goes away.

The back garden looks like a World War One battlefield. Buried somewhere underneath it is Liam's deflated paddling pool.

One night, when Liam is staying with his biological father, Lois and I are drinking and staying up late – at the same time, for once – and Lois sees an advert for a Meat Loaf concert in Manchester. I buy the tickets with what is left on one of my credit cards that has not been consumed by the cost of the extension.

The tickets arrive by email, and I get a nasty feeling that I have been conned. I thought I was buying them from the official box office, but they must have come from an on-line bucket shop. They are for a different day from the one we ordered, and they have someone else's name printed on them. I make various phone calls. The performance is in 3 days. Nobody can help me.

We get the train to Manchester, on one of the hottest days of the year. A load of 'ale trail' men get on at Huddersfield, and are rowdy at first, but Lois and I have got seats, and some Marks & Spencer canned cocktails that we bought at Leeds, and nobody bothers us.

In the queue for customer service at Manchester Arena, I start having an anxiety attack about the validity of the tickets. We queue, and the time when the performance is due to begin gets nearer and nearer. We are the next in line, with about 7 minutes to spare.

A tired-looking Scouser with a moustache explains that the best thing to do with the tickets is to go to the entrance to the auditorium, where they will be scanned, and, if the scanner says we can go in, we are in: if it says we can't go in, there is nothing that can be done about it.

We go into the other queue for the auditorium. I hand over the tickets on the stroke of 8pm, when the concert is due to start. Wrong date. Wrong name. We are let in. Our seats are directly facing the stage, and only about 7 rows from the front. We spend most of the performance on our feet. They are still tuning up when the usher shows us to our seats, and so I go and get a bottle of rosé wine, and two plastic glasses.

The paddling pool ends up in a skip, after Lois and Liam have moved out.

One night, when I am on my own in the under-heated extension, I get talking on Facebook to a woman called Valerie. We send each other messages. On the first night, none of my messages are true. The following morning, she asks me if anything I said was true, and I admit that it was all lies. I apologise. We start again. We announce our relationship. We talk on the phone, a great deal, for a week, and then we meet, at Valerie's house in south east London.

I don't ask Valerie any specific questions. But, if I did, she would get 5 out of 5.

The next tickets for Manchester Arena that I buy are to see Leonard Cohen. It is our first date.

There is no argument about the tickets. The only question is whether our seats will exacerbate Valerie's vertigo. The usher shows us to our places. The seats are fine. We drink a bottle of rosé wine, out of plastic glasses.

Not much more than a year later, Valerie, and her two cats, move to Horbury. Not long after that, we get married. In Gretna. That means that we don't have to invite anybody. The witnesses are Adam and Sarah, from Birmingham. We have never seen them, before, and we don't expect to see them ever again.

We are still trying to work out how to finish paying for the extension, and how to move Valerie's stuff out of storage. Valerie, a lifelong socialist, loves our banners, and our seeming determination to leave nobody behind. She appreciates the prices at our markets.

I still see Liam. I take him to football, and rugby league matches, now and again. I have given him one of my old guitars, and bought him a new amp. I asked him which football team he wanted to see. He said, Leeds United. I asked him which rugby league team he wanted to see. He said, Leeds Rhinos.

Lois and Valerie look after each other's cats, during holidays.

If Liam keeps up with his Spanish, his prospects look zamzastical.

Writers' Biographies

Jimmy Andrex performs all over the UK either with or without music. He has published two collections, Gormless (2011) and Leet (2013), along with three albums of poems to music, Cresties (2015), Puddled & Kallin (2016). Co-Founder (with John Irving Clarke) of Red Shed Readings, he is also compere of Holmfirth's legendary Hot Banana Open Mic and an occasional presenter on elfm's Love the Word. Described by Steve Pottinger as "angry, clever and articulate," his wife thinks he should just tidy up that pile of books next to the bed.

S.J. Bradley is a writer from Leeds, UK, whose short fiction has been published in the US & UK, including in Queen Mobs and in Litro magazine. She is the organiser of DIY literary social Fictions of Every Kind and director of the Northern Short Story Festival. Her second novel, Guest, will be published by Dead Ink Books in June 2017. The story published in this book was previously published in Untitled Books in August 2011. www.sjbradleybooks.blogspot.com

John Irving Clarke is convinced that Hemingway's "one true sentence" is out there somewhere and he will find it by gazing out of windows. Further evidence of his indolence can be found at www.currockpress.com

Steve Dearden was Writer in Residence for the 2013/14 Wakefield Literature Festivals, working with local writers and making the online novella www.wakelost.com. He runs the Writing Squad, developing the next generation of writers in the north. After living in Durham and Yorkshire he has returned to Manchester. www.stevedearden.com

Berlie Doherty writes novels, plays, stories and poetry for all ages, and is translated into over twenty languages. She has written over 60 books, several of which have been dramatised for radio, television and the stage. She has won many awards including the Carnegie Medal twice (Dear Nobody and Granny was a Buffer Girl). Her subjects cover many different genres, from folk and fairy tales and historical fiction to enduring contemporary novels.

Gareth Durasow's poetry has appeared in publications across the UK, Europe and the US. His collection, Endless Running Games, was published by Dog Horn Publishing and featured in The Guardian readers' books of the year. It has been recognised for its "sly charm", "lyrical invention", and the "sheer quality" within its exploration of how video games and the arts use violence to engage their audience. The story featured in this anthology is a little more upbeat.

Ian McMillan is a writer, performer and broadcaster; he presents The Verb each week on BBC Radio 3 and has recently been writing a memoir, poems, song lyrics and libretti for operas.

Silvia Pio is a poet, translator and teacher of English. She co-founded the literary online magazine www.margutte.com, which she co-edits, translating mainly poetry and writing articles and reviews. Silvia also organizes events, such as the global event *100 Thousand Poets for Change* and the poetry exchange Mondovì, Italy-Wakefield, England together with John Irving Clarke. Their poetry collaboration and friendship has continued with the collection *Ondulazioni*, published in 2016.

Laura Potts is a Yorkshire-based poet and has twice been a Foyle Young Poet of the Year. In 2013 she became a Lieder Poet at the

University of Leeds. Currently Editor for Creativity at The Yorker, Laura has also recently become the chosen Young TS Eliot Poet with *Agenda*.

Richard Smyth's short fiction has appeared in journals including *Structo, The Stinging Fly, The Fiction Desk,* and *The Stockholm Review*. His novel *Wild Ink* was published in 2014. He writes for *The Guardian, The TLS, New Statesman* and *The Literary Review,* among others; his latest book, *A Sweet, Wild Note,* is a cultural history of birdsong.

Jane Steele writes, acts and does stand-up comedy, the latter on an intentional basis. Mostly.

Michael Stewart is a writer based in Bradford. His debut novel, *King Crow,* won The Guardian's Not-The-Booker award. His latest novel, *Ill Will,* is to be published by HarperCollins later this year. His debut short fiction collection, *Mr Jolly,* was published by Valley Press last year. He also writes scripts.

Matthew Hedley Stoppard was appointed the first official Otley Town Poet in 2016. He has two collections published by Valley Press, and his poems have featured in magazines, anthologies and on radio and television.

William Thirsk-Gaskill is a writer of short fiction and poetry, and a frequent performer on the West Yorkshire spoken word circuit. His debut poetry collection, *Throwing Mother In The Skip,* is published by Stairwell Books (www.stairwellbooks.co.uk).